Harry Harrison was born in Stamford, Connecticut, grew up in New York City and, promptly on his eighteenth birthday, was drafted into the United States Army. Returning to civilian life some years later, he pursued careers as an artist, art director and editor until, one day, he found himself following a new occupation as free-lance writer. Since then he has lived with his family in more than twenty-seven countries including Mexico, England, Italy and Denmark. The Harrisons now live in Ireland.

By the same author

HARRY HARRISON

War with the Robots

PANTHER
Granada Publishing

Panther Books
Granada Publishing Ltd
8 Grafton Street, London W1X 3LA

Published by Panther Books 1976
Reprinted 1985

First published in Great Britain by
Dobson Books Ltd 1967

ISBN 0-586-04318-7

Printed and bound in Great Britain by
Collins, Glasgow

Set in Linotype Times

For Dan Barry who helped

Contents

A WORD FROM THE (HUMAN) AUTHOR ...

When most people hear the word *robot*, they have a reflexive mental picture of a mechanical man, all creaking joints and glowing eyes. This really wasn't what Karel Capek had in mind when he invented the word for his play *R.U.R.* soon after the First World War. His robots – *Rossum's Universal Robots* – were flesh and blood, though artificially made, and identical with normal placental-people in every way except for their complete lack of emotions. The new word *robot* filled a need, and was gratefully seized by the science fiction writers and soon mutated to become the mechanical man with the steel skin. (Capek's flesh-and-blood robots are now called *androids*.) At the same time, in applied engineering, robot has become an inclusive term for an entire new family of gadgetry.

Just as tools and weapons – hammers, saws, swords and such – are a direct extension of man's physical abilities, robots are an extension of the higher and more abstract functions. The robot pilot, who flies the plane for far longer periods than the human pilot, has delicate powers of discrimination and choice. Even the first crude models could detect and correct deviations from level flight before a human pilot could even sense them, while the newer, sophisticated models turn and bank the plane at the touch of a single button. This process of *sensing and deciding* is what separates the robots from the insensate machines. An alarm clock is a machine – but an automatic clock-radio is a robot. It may not look like one, but it has the functions. It soothes its master to sleep with soft music, then turns off the sound until the correct time in the morning when he should be awakened. There would be no trick at all to en-

larging its field of operation. Instead of a radio this machine could play records: Brahms at night, Sousa in the
morning. And instead of switching off at night after a fixed
interval, the music could continue playing softly until the
master was completely asleep – the robot determining this
fact by a thermocouple in the bed that would detect the
lowering of body temperature that accompanies sleep. If
master wished to arise at dawn there would be no need for
him to check the almanac every night for the correct time; a
simple photoelectric cell sensitive to light would take care
of that. All of these gadgets – instead of being built into a
black box – could be housed in a metal torso, the thermocouple in the end of one finger, the photoelectric cells in
place of eyes. Instead of internal switching it could reach
out a hand to turn on the music, even pull up the shade if
need be.

I personally feel no burning desire to have a truncated
metal man hovering over my bed at night, metal finger
gently prodding my flesh and unsleeping eyes watching for
the sight of dawn. Though in essence it would still be the
same machine that now turns the music on and off for me.

Call my attitude emotional – but don't call it exceptional.
We have long tended to anthropomorphize our mechanical
devices; giving our cars names, cursing, coaxing – and
occasionally kicking – recalcitrant machines. We are even
getting used to the services of robots and are beginning to
take them for granted too. What child has not been fascinated by the moron-level robot in the refrigerator who
turns the light off when we close the door? Does the robot
always turn it off? That train of thought can keep one up
nights figuring out ways to find out.

Have you ever ridden in one of those completely automatic elevators they are beginning to install in the big office
buildings? A single master control starts and stops an entire
bank of elevators, programming frequent trips when the
traffic is heavy and fewer in the slow periods. Passengers
are counted and the doors closed when the car is full. Speed
and braking are adjusted to the weight so that the doors

will always open flush with the floor outside. Some of the elevators even have a recorded voice (appropriately firm) that orders the hoggish rider to stay clear of the door if he is preventing their closure. The elevator-controlling robot is built into the wall and sends and receives all of its commands electronically. If we wanted it to conform to the classic picture of a robot it would do the same job – though perhaps not as efficiently – in the form of a machine man who snapped its fingers at the metal operators of the cars. All of this would be very dramatic, yet would not alter the basic robot-control situation in the slightest.

The robots have arrived and are here to stay, deeply intrenched already in the arts of war and peace. A little antisocial and suicidal robot named proximity-fuse rides in cannon shells and can't stand being next to anyone else. If he is, he blows up. Another robot can dip the bright lights on your car, raising them again when the other car is by, though he is a bit on the stupid side and blinks happily up and down at brightly lit signs. Robot telephone operators are better, cheaper and faster than human ones, though harder to argue with. Robot parking lots have arrived that will whisk your automobile away upon presentation of a coin, and bring it back (hopefully) when you present the right identification. In the home, robot controlled stoves are so commonplace that we take them for granted.

Robots are here to stay all right – but what impact are they going to have on our human society? Will they wreak death and destruction like Victor Frankenstein's creation? Or will they take over the world like their progenitors in *R.U.R.*? Will they be willing serfs or metal masters? Or more subtly, will they assure our physical needs to such a degree that the human race will wallow in slothfulness, degenerate and perish. *Anything's* possible, of course; and in these stories I talk about a few of the possibilities. Some pleasant possibilities, and some rather nasty ones, too. Take your pick....

The first creature from earth to set foot – or treads – onto the moon will be a robot. It is in the design stage now and careful plans are being made for it to stroll around, sample the geology, search for life forms, examine the surface and measure the radiation of the moon. And of course send the information home. Unlike a man, the robot will then peacefully squat down and sit unmoving for all eternity, eye-lenses staring without interest at its home world in the sky above. This little exploration-robot is so attractive a design that it has already caused a schism among the ranks of the scientists as to the necessity of sending men to the moon at all. But I think there is little doubt as to the outcome of the argument. I don't remember any ticker-tape parades for robots. Rockets will reach the moon and the planets and, though there will be many robots aboard, there will also be at least one man. It will be hard to keep him alive, warm and comfortable – but he'll be there. . . .

SIMULATED TRAINER

Mars was a dusty, frigid hell. Bone dry and blood red. They trudged single file through the ankle-deep sand, and in a monotonous duet cursed the nameless engineer who had designed the faulty reconditioners in their pressure suits. The bug hadn't shown during testing of the new suits. It appeared only after they had been using them steadily for a few weeks. The water-absorbers became overloaded and broke down. The Martian atmosphere stood at a frigid $-60°$ centigrade. Inside the suits, they tried to blink the unevaporated sweat from their eyes and slowly cooked in the high humidity.

Morley shook his head viciously to dislodge an itching droplet from his nose. At the same moment, something rust-colored and furry darted across his path. It was the first Martian life they had seen. Instead of scientific curiosity, he felt only anger. A sudden kick sent the animal flying high into the air.

The suddenness of the movement threw him off balance. He fell sideways slowly, dragging his rubberized suit along an upright rock fragment of sharp obsidian.

Tony Bannerman heard the other man's hoarse shout in his earphones and whirled. Morley was down, thrashing on the sand with both hands pressed against the ragged tear in the suit leg. Moisture-laden air was pouring out in a steaming jet that turned instantly to scintillating ice crystals. Tony jumped over to him, trying to seal the tear with his own ineffectual gloves. Their faceplates close, he could see the look of terror on Morley's face – as well as the blue tinge of cyanosis.

'Help me – help me!'

The words were shouted so loud they rasped the tiny helmet earphones. But there was no help. They had taken no emergency patches with them. All the patches were in the ship at least a quarter of a mile away. Before he could get there and back Morley would be dead.

Tony straightened up slowly and sighed. Just the two of them in the ship, there was no one else on Mars who could help. Morley saw the look in Tony's eyes and stopped struggling.

'No hope at all, Tony – I'm dead?'

'Just as soon as all the oxygen is gone; thirty seconds at the most. There's nothing I can do.'

Morley grated the shortest, vilest word he knew and pressed the red EMERGENCY button set into his glove above the wrist. The ground opened up next to him in the same instant, sand sifting down around the edges of the gap. Tony stepped back as two men in white pressure suits came up out of the hole. They had red crosses on the fronts of their helmets and carried a stretcher. They rolled Morley onto it and were gone back into the opening in an instant.

Tony stood looking sourly at the hole for about a minute, waiting until Morley's suit was pushed back through the opening. Then the sand-covered trapdoor closed and the desert was unbroken once more.

The dummy in the suit weighed as much as Morley and its plastic features even resembled him a bit. Some wag had painted black X's on the eyes. *Very funny*, Tony thought, as he struggled to get the clumsy thing onto his back. On the way back the now-quiet Martian animal was lying in his path. He kicked it aside and it rained a fine shower of springs and gears.

The too-small sun was touching the peaks of the saw-tooth red mountains when he reached the ship. Too late for a burial today – it would have to wait until morning. Leaving the thing in the airlock, he stamped into the cabin and peeled off his dripping pressure suit.

It was dark by that time and the things they had called the night-owls began clicking and scratching against the hull of the ship. They had never managed to catch sight of the night-owls; that made the sound doubly annoying. Tony clattered the pans noisily to drown the sound of them out while he prepared the hot evening rations. When the meal was finished and the dishes cleared away, he began to feel the loneliness for the first time. Even the chew of tobacco didn't help; tonight it only reminded him of the humidor of green Havana cigars waiting for him back on earth.

His single kick upset the slim leg of the mess table, sending metal dishes, pans and silverware flying in every direction. They made a satisfactory noise and he exacted even greater pleasure by leaving the mess just that way and going to bed.

They had been so close this time, if only Morley had kept his eyes open! He forced the thought out of his mind and went to sleep.

In the morning he buried Morley. Then, grimly and carefully, passed the remaining two days until blast off time. Most of the geological samples were in and the air sampling and radiation recording meters were fully automatic.

On the final day, he removed the recording tapes from the instruments and carried the instruments away from the ship where they couldn't be caught in the take off blast. Next to the instruments he piled all the extra supplies, machinery and unneeded equipment. Shuffling through the rusty sand for the last time, he gave Morley's grave an ironical salute as he passed. There was nothing to do in the ship and not as much as a pamphlet left to read. Tony passed the two remaining hours on his bunk counting the rivets in the ceiling.

A sharp click from the control clock broke the silence and behind the thick partition he could hear the engines begin the warm-up cycle. At the same time, the padded arms slipped across his bunk, pinning him down securely. He watched the panel slip back in the wall next to him and the hypo arm slide through, moving erratically like a snake as its metal fingers sought him out. They touched his ankle and the serpent's tooth of the needle snapped free. The last thing he saw was the needle slipping into his vein, then the drug blacked him out.

As soon as he was under, a hatch opened in the rear bulkhead and two orderlies brought in a stretcher. They wore no suits nor masks and the blue sky of earth was visible behind them.

Coming to was the same as it always had been. The gentle glow from the stimulants that brought him up out of it, the first sight of the white ceiling of the operating room on earth.

Only this time the ceiling wasn't visible, it was obscured by the red face and thundercloud brow of Colonel Stegham. Tony tried to remember if you saluted while in bed, then decided that the best thing to do was lie quietly.

'Damn it, Bannerman,' the colonel growled, 'welcome back on earth. And why did you bother coming back? With Morley dead the expedition has to be counted a failure – and that means not one completely successful expedition to date.'

'The team in number two, sir, how did they do ...?' Tony tried to sound cheerful.

'Terrible. If anything, worse than your team. Both dead on the second day after landing. A meteor puncture in their oxygen tank and they were too busy discovering a new flora to bother looking at any meters.

'Anyway, that's not why I'm here. Get on some clothes and come into my office.'

He slammed out and Tony scrambled off the bed, ignoring the touch of dizziness from the drugs. When colonels speak, lieutenants hurry to obey.

Colonel Stegham was scowling out of his window when Tony came in. He returned the salute and proved that he had a shard of humanity left in his military soul by offering Tony one of his cigars. Only when they had both lit up did he wave Tony's attention to the field outside the window.

'Do you see that? Know what it is?'

'Yes, sir, the Mars rocket.'

'It's *going* to be the Mars rocket. Right now, it's only a half-completed hull. The motors and instruments are being assembled in plants all over the country. Working on a crash basis the earliest estimate of completion is six months from now.

'The ship will be ready – only we aren't going to have any men to go in her. At the present rate of washout there won't be a single man qualified. Yourself included.'

Tony shifted uncomfortably under his gaze as the colonel continued.

'This training program has always been my baby. I dreamed it up and kept after the Pentagon until it was adapted. We knew we could build a ship that would get to Mars and back, operated by automatic controls that would fly her under any degree of gravity or free fall. But we needed men who could walk out on the surface of the planet and explore it – or the whole thing would be so much wasted effort.

'The ship and the robot pilot could be tested under simulated flight condition, and the bugs worked out. It was my suggestion, which was adopted, that the men who are to go in the ship should be shaken down in the same way. Two pressure chambers were built, simulated trainers that duplicated Mars in every detail we could imagine. We have been running two-men teams through these chambers for eighteen months now, trying to shake down and train them to man the *real* ship out there.

'I'm not going to tell you how many men we started with, or how many have been casualties because of the necessary realism of the chambers. I'll tell you this much though – we haven't had *one successful simulated expedition* in all that time. And every man who has broken down or "died," like your partner Morley, has been eliminated.

'There are only *four* possible men left, yourself included. If we don't get one successful two-man team out of you four, the entire program is a washout.'

Tony sat frozen, the dead cigar between his fingers. He knew that the pressure had been on for some months now, that Colónel Stegham had been growling around like a gunshot bear. The colonel's voice cut through his thoughts.

'Psych division has been after me for what they think is a basic weakness of the program. Their feeling is that because it *is* a training program the men always have it in the back of their minds that it's not for real. They can always be pulled out of a tight hole. Like Morley was, at the last moment. After the results we have had I am beginning to agree with Psych.

'There are four men left and I am going to run one more exercise for each two-man group. This final exercise will be a full dress rehearsal – this time we're playing for keeps.'

'I don't understand, Colonel . . .'

'It's simple.' Stegham accented his words with a bang of his fist on the desk. 'We're not going to help or pull anyone out no matter how much they need it. This is battle training with live ammunition. We're going to throw everything at you that we can think of – and you are going to have to take it. If you tear your suit this time, you're going to die in the Martian vacuum just a few feet from all the air in the world.'

His voice softened just a bit when he dismissed Tony.

'I wish there was some other way to do it, but we have no choice now. We have to get a crew for that ship next month and this is the only way to be sure.'

Tony had a three-day pass. He was drunk the first day, hungover sick the second – and boiling mad on the third. Every man on the project was a volunteer, adding deadly realism that was carrying the thing too far. He could get out any time he wanted, though he knew what he would look like then. There was only one thing to do: go along with the whole stupid idea. He would do what they wanted and go through with it. And when he had finished the exercise, he looked forward to hitting the colonel right on the end of his big bulbous nose.

He joined his new partner, Hal Mendoza, when he went

for his medical. They had met casually at the training lectures before the simulated training began. They shook hands reservedly now, each eyeing the other with a view to future possibilities. It took two men to make a team and either one could be the cause of death for the other.

Mendoza was almost the physical opposite of Tony, tall and wiry, while Tony was as squat and solid as a bear. Tony's relaxed, almost casual manner, was matched by the other man's seemingly tense nerves. Hal chain-smoked and his eyes were never still.

Tony pushed away his momentary worry with an effort. Hal would have to be good to get this far in the program. He would probably calm down once the exercise was under way.

The medic took Tony next and began the detailed examination.

'What's this?' the medical officer asked Tony as he probed with a swab at his cheek.

'Ouch,' Tony said. 'Razor cut, my hand slipped while I was shaving.'

The doctor scowled and painted on antiseptic, then slapped on a square of gauze.

'Watch all skin openings,' he warned. 'They make ideal entry routes for bacteria. Never know what you might find on Mars.'

Tony started a protest, then let it die in his throat. What was the use of explaining that the real trip – if and when it ever came off – would take 260 days. Any cuts would easily heal in that time, even in frozen sleep.

As always after the medical, they climbed into their flight suits and walked over to the testing building. On the way, Tony stopped at the barracks and dug out his chess set and a well-thumbed deck of cards. The access door was open in the thick wall of Building Two and they stepped through into the dummy Mars ship. After the medics had strapped them to the bunks the simulated frozen sleep shots put them under.

*

Coming to was accompanied by the usual nausea and weakness. No realism spared. On a sudden impulse Tony staggered to the latrine mirror and blinked at his red-eyed, smooth-shaven reflection. He tore the bandage off his cheek and his fingers touched the open cut with the still congealed drop of blood at the bottom. A relaxed sigh slipped out. He had the recurrent bad dream that some day one of these training trips would *really* be a flight to Mars. Logic told him that the army would never forego the pleasure and publicity of a big send-off. Yet the doubt, like all illogical ones, persisted. At the beginning of each training flight, he had to abolish it again.

The nausea came back with a swoop and he forced it down. This was one exercise where he couldn't waste time. The ship had to be checked. Hal was sitting up on his bunk waving a limp hand. Tony waved back.

At that moment, the emergency communication speaker crackled into life. At first, there was just the rustle of activity in the control office, then the training officer's voice cut through the background noise.

'Lieutenant Bannerman – you awake yet?'

Tony fumbled the mike out of its clip and reported. 'Here, sir.'

'Just a second, Tony,' the officer said. He mumbled to someone at one side of the mike, then came back on. 'There's been some trouble with one of the bleeder valves in the chamber; the pressure is above Mars norm. Hold the exercise until we pump her back down.'

'Yes, sir,' Tony said, then killed the mike so he and Hal could groan about the so-called efficiency of the training squad. It was only a few minutes before the speaker came back to life.

'Okay, pressure on the button. Carry on as before.'

Tony made an obscene gesture at the unseen man behind the voice and walked over to the single port. He cranked at the handle that moved the crash shield out of the way.

'Well, at least it's a quiet one,' he said after the ruddy

light had streamed in. Hal came up and looked over his shoulder.

'Praise Stegham for that,' he said. 'The last one, where I lost my partner, was wind all the time. From the shape of those dunes it looks like the atmosphere never moves at all.'

They stared glumly at the familiar red landscape and dark sky for a long moment, then Tony turned to the controls while Hal cracked out the atmosphere suits.

'Over here – *quick!*'

Hal didn't have to be called twice, he was at the board in a single jump. He followed Tony's pointing finger.

'The water meter – it shows the tank's only about half full.'

They fought off the plate that gave access to the tank compartment. When they laid it aside a small trickle of rusty water ran across the deck at their feet. Tony crawled in with a flashlight and moved it up and down the tubular tanks. His muffled voice echoed inside the small compartment.

'Damn Stegham and his tricks – another "shock of landing" failure. Connecting pipe split and the water that leaked out has soaked down into the insulating layer; we'll never get it out without tearing the ship apart. Hand me the goo, I'll plug the leak until we can repair it.'

'It's going to be an awfully dry month,' Hal muttered while he checked the rest of the control board.

The first few days were like every other trip. They planted the flag and unloaded the equipment. The observing and recording instruments were set up by the third day, so they unshipped the theodolite and started their maps. By the fourth day they were ready to begin their sample collecting.

It was just at this point that they really became aware of the dust.

Tony chewed an unusually gritty mouthful of rations, cursing under his breath because there was only a mouthful of water to wash it down with. He swallowed it painfully, then looked around the control chamber.

'Have you noticed how dusty it is?' he asked.

'How could you *not* notice it? I have so much of it inside my clothes I feel like I'm living on an ant hill.'

Hal stopped scratching just long enough to take a bite of food.

They both looked around and it hit them for the first time *just* how much dust was in the ship. A red coating on everything, in their food and in their hair. The constant scratch of grit underfoot.

'It must come in on our suits,' Tony said. 'We'll have to clean them off better before coming inside.'

It was a good idea – the only trouble was that it didn't work. The red dust was as fine as talcum powder and no amount of beating could dislodge it; it just drifted around in a fine haze. They tried to forget the dust, just treating it as one more nuisance Stegham's technicians had dreamed up. This worked for awhile, until the eighth day when they couldn't close the outer door of the air lock. They had just returned from a sample-collecting trip. The air lock barely held the two of them plus the bags of rock samples. Taking turns, they beat the dust off each other as well as they could, then Hal threw the cycling switch. The outer door started to close, then stopped. They could feel the increased hum of the door motor through their shoes, then it cut out and the red trouble light flashed on.

'Dust!' Tony said. 'That damned red dust is in the works.'

The inspection plate came off easily and they saw the exposed gear train. The red dust had merged into a destructive mud with the grease. Finding the trouble was easier than repairing it. They had only a few basic tools in their suit pouches. The big tool box and all the solvent that would have made fast work of the job were inside the ship. But they couldn't be reached until the door was fixed. And the door couldn't be fixed without tools. It was a paradoxical situation that seemed very unfunny.

It took them only a second to realize the spot they were

in – and almost two hours to clean the gears as best they could and force the door shut. When the inner port finally opened, both their oxygen tanks read EMPTY, and they were operating on the emergency reserves.

As soon as Hal opened his helmet, he dropped on his bunk. Tony thought he was unconscious until he saw that the other man's eyes were open and staring at the ceiling. He cracked open the single flask of medicinal brandy and forced Hal to take some. Then he had a double swallow himself and tried to ignore the fact that his partner's hands were trembling violently. He busied himself making a better repair of the door mechanism. By the time he had finished, Hal was off the bunk and starting to prepare their evening meal.

Outside of the dust, it was a routine exercise – at first. Surveying and sampling most of the day, then a few leisure hours before retiring. Hal was a good partner and the best chess player Tony had teamed with to date. Tony soon found out that what he thought was nervousness was nervous energy. Hal was only happy when he was doing something. He threw himself into the day's work and had enough enthusiasm and energy left over to smash the yawning Tony over the chessboard. The two men were quite opposite types and made good teammates.

Everything looked good – except for the dust. It was everywhere, and slowly getting into everything. It annoyed Tony, but he stolidly did not let it bother him deeply. Hal was the one that suffered most. It scratched and itched him, setting his temper on edge. He began to have trouble sleeping.

And the creeping dust was slowly working its way into every single item of equipment. The machinery was starting to wear as fast as their nerves. The constant presence of the itching dust, together with the acute water shortage was maddening. They were always thirsty and had only the minimum amount of water to last until blast off. With proper rationing, it would barely be enough.

They quarreled over the ration on the thirteenth day and

almost came to blows. For two days after that they didn't talk. Tony noticed that Hal always kept one of the sampling hammers in his pocket; in turn, he took to carrying one of the dinner knives.

Something had to crack. It turned out to be Hal.

It must have been the lack of sleep that finally got to him. He had always been a light sleeper, now the tension and the dust were too much. Tony could hear him scratching and turning each night when he forced himself to sleep. He wasn't sleeping too well himself, but at least he managed to get a bit. From the black hollows under Hal's bloodshot eyes it didn't look like Hal was getting any.

On the eighteenth day he cracked. They were just getting into their suits when he started shaking. Not just his hands, but all over. He just stood there shaking until Tony got him to the bunk and gave him the rest of the brandy. When the attack was over he refused to go outside.

'I won't ... *I can't!*' He screamed the words. 'The suits won't last much longer, they'll fail while we're out there ... *I* won't last any longer ... we have to go back ...'

Tony tried to reason with him. 'We can't do that, you know this is a full-scale exercise. We can't get out until the twenty-eight days are up. That's only ten more days – you can hold out until then. That's the minimum figure the army decided on for a stay on Mars – it's built into all the plans and machinery. Be glad we don't have to wait an entire Martian year until the planets get back into conjunction. With deep sleep and atomic drive that's one trouble that won't be faced.'

'Stop talking and trying to kid me along,' Hal shouted. 'I don't give a flying frog what happens to the first expedition. I'm washing myself out and this final exercise will go right with me. I'm not going crazy from lack of sleep just because some brass-hat thinks super-realism is the answer. If they refuse to stop the exercise when I call, it will be *murder*.'

He was out of his bunk before Tony could say anything and scratching at the control board. The EMERGENCY button was there as always, but they didn't know if it was connected this time. Or even if it were connected, if anyone would answer. Hal pushed it and kept pushing it. They both looked at the speaker, holding their breaths.

'The dirty rotten ... they're not going to answer the call.' Hal barely breathed the words.

Then the speaker rasped to life and the cold voice of Colonel Stegham filled the tiny room.

'You know the conditions of this exercise – so your reasons for calling had better be pretty good. What are they?'

Hal grabbed the microphone, half-complaining, half-pleading – the words poured out in a torrent. As soon as he started, Tony knew it would not be any good. He knew just how Stegham would react to the complaints. While Hal was still pleading the speaker cut him off.

'That's enough. Your explanation doesn't warrant any change in the original plan. You are on your own and you're going to have to stay that way. I'm cutting this connection permanently; don't attempt to contact me again until the exercise is over.'

The click of the opening circuit was as final as death.

Hal sat dazed, tears on his cheeks. It wasn't until he stood up that Tony realized they were tears of anger. With a single pull, Hal yanked the mike loose and heaved it through the speaker grill.

'Wait until this is over, Colonel, and I can get your pudgy neck between my hands.' He whirled towards Tony. 'Get out the medical kit, I'll show that idiot he's not the only one who can play boyscout with his damned exercises.'

There were four morphine styrettes in the kit; he grabbed one out, broke the seal and jabbed it against his arm. Tony didn't try to stop him, in fact, he agreed with him completely. Within a few minutes, Hal was slumped over the table, snoring deeply. Tony picked him up and dropped him onto his bunk.

Hal slept almost twenty hours and when he woke up some of the madness and exhaustion was gone from his eyes. Neither of them mentioned what had happened. Hal marked the days remaining on the bulkhead and carefully rationed the remaining morphine. He was getting about one night's sleep in three, but it seemed to be enough.

They had four days left to blast off when Tony found the first Martian life. It was something about the size of a cat that crouched in the lee of the ship, He called to Hal who came over and looked at it.

'That's a beauty,' he said, 'but nowheres near as good as the one I had on my second trip. I found this ropy thing that oozed a kind of glue. Contrary to regulations – frankly I was curious as hell – I dissected the thing. It was a beauty, all wheels and springs and gears, Stegham's technicians do a good job. I really got chewed out for opening the thing, though. Why don't we just leave this one where it is?'

For a moment Tony almost agreed – then changed his mind.

'That's probably just what they want – so let's finish the game their way. I'll watch it, you get one of the empty ration cartons.'

Hal reluctantly agreed and climbed into the ship. The outer door swung slowly and ground into place. Disturbed by the vibration, the thing darted out towards Tony. He gasped and stepped back before he remembered it was only a robot.

'Those technicians really have wonderful imaginations,' he mumbled.

The thing started to run by him and he put his foot on some of its legs to hold it. There were plenty of legs; it was like a small-bodied spider surrounded by a thousand unarticulated legs. They moved in undulating waves like a milliped and dragged the misshapen body across the sand. Tony's boot crunched on the legs, tearing some off. The rest held.

Being careful to keep his hand away from the churning legs, he bent over and picked up a dismembered limb. It was hard and covered with spines on the bottom side. A milky fluid was dripping from the torn end.

'Realism,' he said to himself, 'those technicians sure believe in realism.'

And then the thought hit him. A horribly impossible thought that froze the breath in his throat. The thoughts whirled round and round and he knew they were wrong because they were so incredible. Yet he had to find out, even if it meant ruining their mechanical toy.

Keeping his foot carefully on the thing's legs, he slipped the sharpened table knife out of his pouch and bent over. With a single, swift motion he stabbed.

'What the devil are you doing?' Hal asked, coming up behind him. Tony couldn't answer and he couldn't move. Hal walked around him and looked down at the thing on the ground.

It took him a second to understand, then he screamed.

'*It's alive!* It's bleeding and there are no gears inside. It can't be alive – if it is we're not on earth at all – *we're on Mars!*' He began to run, then fell down, screaming.

Tony thought and acted at the same time. He knew he only had one chance. If he missed they'd both be dead. Hal would kill them both in his madness. Balling his fist, he let swing hard as he could at the spot just under the other man's breastplate. There was just the thin fabric of the suit there and that spot was right over the big nerve ganglion of the solar plexus. The thud of the blow hurt his hand – but Hal collapsed slowly to the ground. Putting his hands under the other's arms, he dragged him into the ship.

Hal started to come to after he had stripped him and laid him on the bunk. It was impossible to hold him down with one hand and press the freeze cycling button at the same time. He concentrated on holding Hal's one leg still and pushed the button. The crazed man had time to hit Tony three times before the needle lanced home. He dropped back with a sigh and Tony got groggily to his feet. The manual actuator on the frozen sleep had been provided for any medical emergency so the patient could survive until the doctors could work on him back at base. It had proved its value.

Then the same unreasoning terror hit him.

If the beast were real – Mars was real.

This was no 'training exercise' – this was it. That sky outside wasn't a painted atmosphere, it was the real sky of Mars. He was alone as no man had ever been alone before. On a planet millions of miles from his world.

He was shouting as he dogged home the outer air lock door, an animal-like howl of a lost beast. He had barely enough control left to get to his bunk and throw the switch above it. The hypodermic was made of good steel so it went right through the fabric of his pressure suit. He was just reaching for the hypo arm to break it off when he dropped off into the blackness.

This time, he was slow to open his eyes. He was afraid he would see the riveted hull of the ship above his head. It was the white ceiling of the hospital, though, and he let the captive air out of his lungs. When he turned his head he saw Colonel Stegham sitting by the bed.

'Did we make it?' Tony asked. It was more of a statement than a question.

'You made it, Tony. Both of you made it. Hal is awake here in the other bed.'

There was something different about the colonel's voice and it took Tony an instant to recognize it. It was the first time he had ever heard the colonel talk with any emotion other than anger.

'The first trip to Mars. You can imagine what the papers are saying about it. More important, Tech says the specimens and meter reading you brought back are invaluable. When did you find out it wasn't an exercise?'

'The twenty-fourth day. We found some kind of Martian animal. I suppose we were pretty stupid not to have tumbled before that.'

Tony's voice had an edge of bitterness.

'Not really. Every part of your training was designed to keep you from finding out. We were never certain if we would have to send the men without their knowledge, but there was always that possibility. Psych was sure the disorientation and separation from earth would cause a breakdown. I could never agree with them.'

'They were right,' Tony said, trying to keep the memory of fear out of his voice.

'We know now they were right, though I fought them at the time. Psych won the fight and we programmed the whole trip over on their say-so. I doubt if you appreciate it, but we went to a tremendous amount of work to convince you two that you were still in the training program.'

'Sorry to put you to all that trouble,' Hal said. The colonel flushed a little, not at the words but at the looselyreined bitterness that rode behind them. He went on as if he hadn't heard.

'Those two conversations you had over the emergency phone were, of course, taped and the playback concealed in the ship. Psych scripted them on the basis of fitting any need, apparently they worked. The second one was supposed to be the final touch of realism, in case you should start being doubtful. Then we used a variation of deep freeze that suspends about ninety-nine per cent of the body processes; it hasn't been revealed or published yet. This along with anticoagulents in the razor cut on Tony's chin covered the fact that so much time had passed.'

'What about the ship,' Hal asked. 'We saw it – it was only half-completed.'

'Dummy,' the colonel said. 'Put there for the public's benefit and all foreign intelligence services. Real one had been finished and tested weeks earlier. Getting the crew was the difficult part. What I said about no team finishing a practice exercise was true. You two men had the best records and were our best bets.

'We'll never have to do it this way again, though. Psych says that the next crews won't have that trouble; they'll be reinforced by the psychological fact that someone else was there before them. They won't be facing the complete unknown.'

The colonel sat chewing his lip for a moment, then forced

out the words he had been trying to say since Tony and Hal had regained consciousness.

'I want you to understand ... both of you ... that I would rather have gone myself than pull that kind of thing on you. I know how you must feel. Like we pulled some kind of a ...'

'Interplanetary practical joke,' Tony said. He didn't smile when he said it.

'Yes, something like that,' the colonel rushed on. 'I guess it was a lousy trick – but don't you see, we had to? You two were the only ones left, every other man had washed out. It had to be you two, and we had to do it the safest way.

'And only myself and three other men know what was done; what really happened on the trip. No one else will ever know about it, I can guarantee you that.'

Hal's voice was quiet, but cut through the still room like a sharp knife.

'You can be sure Colonel, that *we* won't be telling anybody about it.'

When Colonel Stegham left, he kept his head down because he couldn't bring himself to see the look in the eyes of the first two explorers of Mars.

Sooner or later robots will be built that will fulfill the physical prophecies of fiction. The human body with its binocular vision and highly placed eyes, dextrous fingers placed at the ends of long and flexible extremities, and two-legged motive power for any kind of terrain, will surely be used as a pattern for the construction of robots. They will be machines that look like men – but they will not be metal men. This is not an easy distinction to make, and an even easier one to forget, as we do every time we strike out in anger at an inanimate object. But robots will not be inanimate, in truth they will be animate in every way. They will be *man-shaped* machines – and people will begin to think of them as another class of mankind. . . .

THE VELVET GLOVE

Jon Venex fitted the key into the hotel room door. He had asked for a large room, the largest in the hotel, and had paid the desk clerk extra for it. All he could do now was pray that he hadn't been cheated. He wouldn't dare complain or try to get his money back. He heaved a sigh of relief as the door swung open. The room was bigger than he had expected – fully three feet wide by five feet long. There was more than enough space to work in. He would have his leg off in a jiffy and by morning his limp would be gone.

There was the usual adjustable hook on the back wall. He slipped it through the recessed ring in the back of his neck and kicked himself up until his feet hung free of the floor. His legs relaxed with a rattle as he cut off all power below his waist.

The overworked leg motor would have to cool down before he could work on it, plenty of time to skim through the newspaper. With the chronic worry of the unemployed he snapped it open at the want-ads and ran his eye down the *Help Wanted – Robot* column. There was nothing for him under the Specialist heading, even the Unskilled Labor listings were bare and unpromising. New York was a bad town for robots this year.

The want-ads were just as depressing as usual but he could always get a lift from the comic section. He even had a favorite strip, a fact that he scarcely dared mention to himself – 'Rattly Robot,' a dull-witted mechanical clod who was continually falling over himself and getting into trouble. It was a repellent caricature, but could still be very funny. Jon was just starting to read it when the ceiling light went out.

It was ten P.M., curfew hour for robots. Lights out and lock yourself in until six in the morning, eight hours of boredom and darkness for all except the few night workers. But there were ways of getting around the letter of a law that didn't concern itself with a definition of visible light. Sliding aside some of the shielding around his atomic generator, Jon turned up the gain. As it began to run a little hot the heat waves streamed out – visible to him as infrared rays. He finished reading the paper in the clear light of his abdomen.

With the thermocouple in the tip of his second finger left hand, he tested the temperature of his leg. It was cool enough to work on. The waterproof gasket stripped off easily, exposing the power leads, nerve wires and the weakened knee joint. The wires disconnected, Jon unscrewed the knee above the joint and carefully placed it on the shelf in front of him. With loving care he took the replacement part from his hip pouch. It was the product of toil, purchased with the savings from three months' employment on the Jersey pig farm.

Jon was standing on one leg testing the new knee joint when the ceiling fluorescent flickered and came back on. Five-thirty already, he had just finished in time. A shot of oil on the new bearing completed the job; he stowed away the tools in his pouch and unlocked the door.

The unused elevator shaft acted as a waste chute, he slipped his newspaper through a slot in the door as he went by. Keeping close to the wall, he picked his way carefully down the grease-stained stairs. He slowed his pace at the 17th floor as two other mechs turned in ahead of him. They were obviously butchers or meatcutters; where the right hand should have been on each of them there stuck out a wicked, foot-long knife. As they approached the foot of the stairs they stopped to slip the knives into the plastic sheaths that were bolted to their chestplates. Jon followed them down the ramp into the lobby.

The room was filled to capacity with robots of all sizes, forms and colors. Jon Venex's greater height enabled him to see over their heads to the glass doors that opened onto the street. It had rained the night before and the rising sun drove red glints from the puddles on the sidewalk. Three robots, painted snow white to show they were night workers, pushed the doors open and came in. No one went out as the curfew hadn't ended yet. They milled around, slowly talking in low voices.

The only human being in the entire lobby was the night clerk dozing behind the counter. The clock over his head said five minutes to six. Shifting his glance from the clock Jon became aware of a squat black robot waving to attract his attention. The powerful arms and compact build identified him as a member of the Diger family, one of the largest groups. He pushed through the crowd and clapped Jon on the back with a resounding clang.

'Jon Venex! I knew it was you as soon as I saw you sticking up out of this crowd like a green tree trunk. I haven't seen you since the old days on Venus!'

Jon didn't need to check the number stamped on the short one's scratched chestplate. Alec Diger had been his only close friend during those thirteen boring years at Orange Sea Camp. A good chess player and a whiz at Two-handed Handball, they had spent all their off time together. They shook hands, with the extra squeeze that means friendliness.

'Alec, you beat-up little grease pot, what brings you to New York?'

'The burning desire to see something besides rain and jungle, if you must know. After you bought-out, things got just too damn dull. I began working two shifts a day in that foul diamond mine, and then three a day for the last month to get enough credits to buy my contract and passage back to earth. I was underground so long that the photocell on my right eye burned out when the sunlight hit it.'

He leaned forward with a hoarse confidential whisper, 'If you want to know the truth, I had a sixty carat diamond stuck behind the eye lens. I sold it here on earth for two hundred credits, gave me six months of easy living. It's all gone now, so I'm on my way to the employment exchange. His voice boomed loud again, 'And how about *you*?'

'It's just been the old routine with me, a run of odd jobs until I got side-swiped by a bus – it fractured my knee bearing. The only job I could get with a bad leg was feeding slops to pigs. Earned enough to fix the knee – and here I am.'

Alec jerked his thumb at a rust colored, three-foot tall robot that had come up quietly beside him. 'If you think you've got trouble take a look at Dik here. That's no coat of paint on him. Dik Dryer, meet Jon Venex an old buddy of mine.'

Jon bent over to shake the little mech's hand. His eye shutters dilated as he realized what he had thought was a coat of paint was a thin layer of rust that coated Dik's metal body. Alec scratched a shiny path in the rust with his finger tip. His voice was suddenly serious.

'Dik was designed for operation in the Martian desert. It's as dry as a fossil bone there so his skinflint company cut corners on the stainless steel.

'When they went bankrupt he was sold to a firm here in the city. After awhile the rust started to eat in and slow him down, they gave Dik his contract and threw him out.'

The small robot spoke for the first time, his voice grated and scratched. 'Nobody will hire me like this, but I can't get repaired until I get a job.' His arms squeaked and grated as he moved them. 'I'm going by the Robot Free Clinic again today, they said they might be able to do something.'

Alec Diger rumbled in his deep chest. 'Don't put too much faith in those people. They're great at giving out tenth-credit oil capsules or a little free wire – but don't depend on them for anything important.'

It was six now, the robots were pushing through the doors into the silent streets. They joined the crowd moving out, Jon slowing his stride so his shorter friends could keep pace. Dik Dryer moved with a jerking, irregular motion, his voice as uneven as the motion of his body.

'Jon – Venex, I don't recognize your family name. Something to do – with Venus – perhaps.'

'Venus is right, Venus Experimental – there are only twenty-two of us in the family. We have water-proof, pressure-resistant bodies for working down on the ocean bottom. The basic idea was all right, we did our part, only there wasn't enough money in the channel-dredging contract to keep us all working. I bought out my original contract at half price and became a free robot.'

Dik vibrated his rusted diaphragm. 'Being free isn't all it should be. I some – times wish the Robot Equality Act hadn't been passed. I would just l-love to be owned by a nice rich company with a machine shop and a – mountain of replacement parts.'

'You don't really mean that Dik,' Alec Diger clamped a heavy black arm across his shoulders. 'Things aren't perfect now, we know that, but it's certainly a lot better than the old days. We were just hunks of machinery then, used twenty-four hours a day until we were worn out and then thrown in the junk pile. No thanks, I'll take my chances with things as they are.'

Jon and Alec turned into the employment exchange, saying good-by to Dik who went on slowly down the street. They pushed up the crowded ramp and joined the line in front of the registration desk. The bulletin board next to the desk held a scattering of white slips announcing job openings. A clerk was pinning up new additions.

Venex scanned them with his eyes, stopping at one circled in red.

ROBOTS NEEDED IN THESE CATEGORIES. APPLY AT ONCE TO CHAINJET, LTD., 1219 BROADWAY
    Fasten
    Flyer
    Atommel
    Filmer
    Venex

Jon rapped excitedly on Alec Diger's neck. 'Look there, a job in my own specialty – I can get my old pay rate! See you back at the hotel tonight – and good luck in your job hunting.'

Alec waved good-by. 'Let's hope the job's as good as you think, I never trust those things until I have my credits in my hand.'

Jon walked quickly from the employment exchange, his long legs eating up the blocks. *Good old Alec, he didn't believe in anything he couldn't touch. Perhaps he was right, but why try to be unhappy. The world wasn't too bad this morning – his leg worked fine, prospects of a good job – he hadn't felt this cheerful since the day he was activated.*

Turning the corner at a brisk pace he collided with a human coming from the opposite direction. Jon had stopped on the instant, but there wasn't time to jump aside. The fat man jarred against him and fell to the ground. From the height of elation to the depths of despair in an instant – he had injured a *human being*!

He bent to help the man to his feet, but the other would have none of that. He evaded the friendly hand and screeched in a high-pitched voice.

'Officer, officer-police ... *help!* I've been attacked – a mad robot ... *help!*'

A crowd was gathering – staying at a respectful distance – but making an angry muttering noise. Jon stood motionless, his head reeling at the enormity of what he had done. A policeman pushed his way through the crowd.

'Seize him officer, shoot him down ... he struck me ... almost killed me ...' The man shook with rage, his words thickening to a senseless babble.

The policeman had his .75 recoilless revolver out and pressed against Jon's side.

'This *man* has charged you with a serious crime, *greasecan*. I'm taking you into the stationhouse – to talk about it.' He looked around nervously, waving his gun to open a path through the tightly packed crowd. They moved back grudgingly, with murmurs of disapproval.

Jon's thoughts swirled in tight circles. How did a catastrophe like this happen, where was it going to end? He didn't dare tell the truth, that would mean he was calling the man a liar. There had been six robots power-lined in the city since the first of the year. If he dared speak in his own defense there would be a jumper to the street lighting circuit and a seventh burnt out hulk in the police morgue.

A feeling of resignation swept through him, there was no way out. If the man pressed charges it would mean a term of penal servitude, though it looked now as if he would never live to reach the court. The papers had been whipping up a lot of anti-robe feeling, you could feel it behind the angry voices, see it in the narrowed eyes and clenched fists. The crowd was slowly changing into a mob, a mindless mob as yet, but capable of turning on him at any moment.

'What's going on here ...?', it was a booming voice, with a quality that dragged at the attention of the crowd.

A giant cross-continent freighter was parked at the curb. The driver swung down from the cab and pushed his way through the people. The policeman shifted his gun as the man strode up to him.

'That's my robot you got there Jack, don't put any holes in him!' He turned on the man who had been shouting accusations. 'Fatty here, is the world's biggest liar. The robot was standing here waiting for me to park the truck. Fatty must be as blind as he is stupid, I saw the whole thing. He knocks himself down walking into the robe, then starts hollering for the cops.'

The other man could take no more. His face crimson with anger he rushed toward the trucker, his fists swinging in ungainly circles. They never landed, the truck driver put a meaty hand on the other's face and seated him on the sidewalk for the second time.

The onlookers roared with laughter, the power-lining and the robot were forgotten. The fight was between two men now, the original cause had slipped from their minds. Even the policeman allowed himself a small smile as he holstered his gun and stepped forward to separate the men.

The trucker turned towards Jon with a scowl.

'Come on you aboard the truck – you've caused me enough trouble for one day. What a junkcan!'

The crowd chuckled as he pushed Jon ahead of him into the truck and slammed the door behind them. Jamming the starter with his thumb he gunned the thunderous diesels into life and pulled out into the traffic.

Jon moved his jaw, but there were no words to come out. Why had this total stranger helped him, what could he say to show his appreciation? He knew that all humans weren't robe-haters, why it was even rumored that some humans treated robots as *equals* instead of machines. The driver must be one of these mythical individuals, there was no other way to explain his actions.

Driving carefully with one hand the man reached up behind the dash and drew out a thin, plastikoid booklet. He handed it to Jon who quickly scanned the title, *Robot Slaves in a World Economy*, by Philpott Asimov II.

'If you're caught reading that thing they'll execute you on the spot. Better stick it between the insulation and your generator, you can always burn it if you're picked up.

'Read it when you're alone, it's got a lot of things in it that you know nothing about. Robots aren't really inferior to humans, in fact they're superior in most things. There is even a little history in there to show that robots aren't the first ones to be treated as second-class citizens. You may find it a little hard to believe, but human beings once treated each other just the way they treat robots now. That's one of the reasons I'm active in this movement – sort of like the fellow who was burned helping others stay away from the fire.'

His smile was friendly, the whiteness of his teeth standing out against the rich ebony brown of his features.

'I'm heading towards US-1, can I drop you anywheres on the way?'

'The Chainjet Building please – I'm applying for a job.'

They rode the rest of the way in silence. Before he opened the door the driver shook hands with Jon.

'Sorry about calling you *Junkcan*, but the crowd expected it.' He didn't look back as he drove away.

Jon had to wait a half hour for his turn, but the receptionist finally signalled him towards the door of the interviewer's room. He stepped in quickly and turned to face the man seated at the transplastic desk, an upset little man with permanent worry wrinkles stamped in his forehead. The little man shoved the papers on the desk around angrily, occasionally making crabbed little notes on the margins. He flashed a birdlike glance up at Jon.

'Yes, yes, be quick. What is it you want?'

'You posted a help wanted notice, I—'

The man cut him off with a wave of his hand. 'All right let me see your ID tag ... quickly, there are others waiting.'

Jon thumbed the tag out of his waist slot and handed it across the desk. The interviewer read the code number, then began running his finger down a long list of similar figures. He stopped suddenly and looked sideways at Jon from under his lowered lids.

'You have made a mistake, we have no opening for you.'

Jon began to explain to the man that the notice had requested his specialty, but he was waved to silence. As the interviewer handed back the tag he slipped a card out from under the desk blotter and held it in front of Jon's eyes. He held it there for only an instant, knowing that the written message was recorded instantly by the robot's photographic vision and eidetic memory. The card dropped into the ash tray and flared into embers at the touch of the man's pencil-heater.

Jon stuffed the ID tag back into the slot and read over the message on the card as he walked down the stairs to the street. There were six lines of typewritten copy with no signature.

To Venex Robot: You are urgently needed on a top secret company project. There are suspected informers in the main office, so you are being hired in this unusual manner. Go at once to 787 Washington Street and ask for Mr. Coleman.

Jon felt an immense sensation of relief. For a moment there, he was sure the job had been a false lead. He saw nothing unusual in the method of hiring. The big corporations were immensely jealous of their research discoveries and went to great lengths to keep them secret – at the same time resorting to any means to ferret out their business rivals' secrets. There might still be a chance to get this job.

The burly bulk of a lifter was moving back and forth in the gloom of the ancient warehouse stacking crates in ceiling-high rows. Jon called to him, the robot swung up his forklift and rolled over on noiseless tires. When Jon questioned him he indicated a stairwell against the rear wall.

'Mr. Coleman's office is down in back, the door is marked.' The lifter put his fingertips against Jon's ear pickups and lowered his voice to the merest shadow of a whisper. It would have been inaudible to human ears, but Jon could hear him easily, the sounds being carried through the metal of the other's body.

'He's the meanest man you ever met – he hates robots, so be *ever* so polite. If you can use "sir" five times in one sentence you're perfectly safe.'

Jon swept the shutter over one eye tube in a conspiratorial wink, the large mech did the same as he rolled away. Jon turned and went down the dusty stairwell and knocked gently on Mr. Coleman's door.

Coleman was a plump little individual in a conservative purple and yellow business suit. He kept glancing from Jon to the Robot General Catalog checking the Venex specifications listed there. Seemingly satisfied he slammed the book shut.

'Gimme your tag and back against that wall to get measured.'

Jon laid his ID tag on the desk and stepped towards the

wall. 'Yes sir, here it is sir.' Two 'sirs' on that one, not bad for the first sentence. He wondered idly if he could put five of them in one sentence without the man knowing he was being made a fool of.

He became aware of the danger an instant too late. The current surged through the powerful electromagnet behind the plaster flattening his metal body helplessly against the wall. Coleman was almost dancing with glee.

'We got him Druce, he's mashed flatter than a stinking tin-can on a rock, can't move a motor. Bring that junk in here and let's get him ready.'

Druce had a mechanic's coveralls on over his street suit and a tool box slung under one arm. He carried a little black metal can at arm's length, trying to get as far from it as possible. Coleman shouted at him with annoyance.

'That bomb can't go off until it's armed, stop acting like a child. Put it on that grease-can's leg and *quick*!'

Grumbling under his breath Druce spot-welded the metal flanges of the bomb onto Jon's leg a few inches above his knee. Coleman tugged at it to be certain it was secure, then twisted a knob in the side and pulled out a glistening length of pin. There was a cold little click from inside the mechanism as it armed itself.

Jon could do nothing except watch, even his vocal diaphragm was locked by the magnetic field. He had more than a suspicion however that he was involved in something other than a 'secret business deal.' He cursed his own stupidity for walking blindly into the situation.

The magnetic field cut off and he instantly raced his extensor motors to leap forward. Coleman took a plastic box out of his pocket and held his thumb over a switch inset into its top.

'Don't make any quick moves junk-yard, this little transmitter is keyed to a receiver in that bomb on your leg. One touch of my thumb, up you go in a cloud of smoke and come down in a shower of nuts and bolts.' He signalled to Druce who opened a closet door. 'And in case you want to be heroic, just think of him.'

Coleman jerked his thumb at the sodden shape on the floor; a filthily attired man of indistinguishable age whose only interesting feature was the black bomb strapped tightly across his chest. He peered unseeingly from red-rimmed eyes and raised the almost empty whiskey bottle to his mouth. Coleman kicked the door shut.

'He's just some Bowery bum we dragged in, Venex, but that doesn't make any difference to you, does it? He's human – and a robot can't kill *anybody*! That rummy has a bomb on him tuned to the same frequency as yours, if you don't play ball with us he gets a two-foot hole blown in his chest.'

Coleman was right, Jon didn't dare make any false moves. All of his early mental training as well as Circuit 92 sealed inside his brain case would prevent him from harming a human being. He felt trapped, caught by these people for some unknown purpose.

Coleman had pushed back a tarpaulin to disclose a ragged hole in the concrete floor, the opening extended into the earth below. He waved Jon over.

'The tunnel is in good shape for about thirty feet, then you'll find a fall. Clean all the rock and dirt out until you break through into the storm sewer, then come back. And you better be alone. If you tip the cops both you and the old stew go out together – now move.'

The shaft had been dug recently and shored with packing crates from the warehouse overhead. It ended abruptly in a wall of fresh sand and stone. Jon began shoveling it into the little wheelbarrow they had given him.

He had emptied four barrow loads and was filling the fifth when he uncovered the hand, a robot's hand made of green metal. He turned his headlight power up and examined the hand closely, there could be no doubt about it. These gaskets on the joints, the rivet pattern at the base of the thumb meant only one thing, it was the dismembered hand of a Venex robot.

Quickly, yet gently, he shoveled away the rubble behind the hand and unearthed the rest of the robot. The torso was crushed and the power circuits shorted, battery acid was dripping from an ugly rent in the side. With infinite care Jon snapped the few remaining wires that joined the neck to the body and laid the green head on the barrow. It stared at him like a skull, the shutters completely dilated, but no glow of life from the tubes behind them.

He was scraping the mud from the number on the battered chestplate when Druce lowered himself into the tunnel and flashed the brilliant beam of a hand-spot down its length.

'Stop playing with that junk and get digging – or you'll end up the same as him. This tunnel has gotta be through by tonight.'

Jon put the dismembered parts on the barrow with the sand and rock and pushed the whole load back up the tunnel, his thoughts running in unhappy circles. A dead robot was a terrible thing, and one of his family too. But there was something wrong about this robot, something that was quite inexplicable, the number on the plate had been '17,' yet he remembered only too well the day that a water-shorted motor had killed Venex 17 in the Orange Sea.

It took Jon four hours to drive the tunnel as far as the ancient granite wall of the storm sewer. Druce gave him a short pinch bar and he levered out enough of the big blocks to make a hole large enough to let him through into the sewer.

When he climbed back into the office he tried to look casual as he dropped the pinch bar to the floor by his feet and seated himself on the pile of rubble in the corner. He moved around to make a comfortable seat for himself and his fingers grabbed the severed neck of Venex 17.

Coleman swiveled around in his chair and squinted at the wall clock. He checked the time against his tie-pin watch, with a grunt of satisfaction he turned back and stabbed a finger at Jon.

'Listen you green junk-pile, at 1900 hours you're going to do a job, and there aren't going to be any slip-ups. You go down that sewer and into the Hudson River. The outlet is under water, so you won't be seen from the docks. Climb down to the bottom and walk 200 yards north, that should put you just under a ship. Keep your eyes open, *but don't show any lights!* About halfway down the keel of the ship you'll find a chain hanging.

'Climb the chain, pull loose the box that's fastened there to the hull and bring it back here. No mistakes – or you know what happens.'

Jon nodded his head. His busy fingers had been separating the wires in the amputated neck. When they had been straightened and put into a row he memorized their order with one flashing glance.

He ran over the color code in his mind and compared it with the memorized leads. The twelfth wire was the main cranial power lead, number six was the return wire.

With his precise touch he separated these two from the pack and glanced idly around the room. Druce was dozing on a chair in the opposite corner, Coleman was talking on the phone, his voice occasionally rising in a petulant whine. This wasn't interfering with his attention to Jon – and the radio switch still held tightly in his left hand.

Jon's body blocked Coleman's vision, as long as Druce stayed asleep he would be able to work on the head unobserved. He activated a relay in his forearm and there was a click as the waterproof cover on an exterior socket swung open. This was a power outlet from his battery that was used to operate motorized tools and lights underwater.

If Venex 17's head had been severed for less than three weeks he could reactivate it. Every robot had a small storage battery inside his skull, if the power to the brain was cut off the battery would provide the minimum standby current to keep the brain alive. The robe would be unconscious until full power was restored.

Jon plugged the wires into his arm-outlet and slowly raised the current to operating level. There was a tense moment of waiting, then 17's eye shutters suddenly closed. When they opened again the eye tubes were glowing warmly. They swept the room with one glance then focused on Jon.

The right shutter clicked shut while the other began opening and closing in rapid fashion. It was International code – being sent as fast as the solenoid could be operated. Jon concentrated on the message.

Telephone – call emergency operator – tell her 'signal 14' help will – The shutter stopped in the middle of a code group, the light of reason dying from the eyes.

For one instant Jon knew panic, until he realized that 17 had deliberately cut the power. Druce's harsh voice rasped in his ear.

'What you doing with that? None of your funny robot tricks, I know your kind, plotting all kinds of things in them tin domes.' His voice trailed off into a stream of incomprehensible profanity. With sudden spite he lashed his foot out and sent 17's head crashing against the wall.

The dented, green head rolled to a stop at Jon's feet, the face staring up at him in mute agony. It was only Circuit 92 that prevented him from injuring a *human*. As his motors revved up to send him hurtling forward the control relays clicked open. He sank against the debris, paralyzed for the instant. As soon as the rush of anger was gone he would regain control of his body.

They stood as if frozen in a tableau. The robot slumped backward, the man leaning forward, his face twisted with unreasoning hatred. The head lay between them like a symbol of death.

Coleman's voice cut through the air of tenseness like a knife.

'*Druce*. stop playing with the grease-can and get down to the main door to let Little Willy and his Junk-brokers in. You can have it all to yourself afterward.'

The angry man turned reluctantly, but pushed out of the door at Coleman's annoyed growl. Jon sat down against the walls, his mind sorting out the few facts with instantaneous precision. There was no room in his thoughts for Druce, the man had become just one more factor in a complex problem.

Call the emergency operator – that meant this was no local matter, responsible authorities must be involved. Only the government could be behind a thing as major as this. Signal 14 – that implied a complex set of arrangements, forces that could swing into action at a moment's notice. There was no indication where this might lead, but the only thing to do was to get out of here and make that phone call. And quickly. Druce was bringing in more people, junk-brokers, whatever they were. Any action that he took would have to be done before they returned.

Even as Jon followed this train of logic his fingers were busy. Palming a wrench, he was swiftly loosening the main retaining nut on his hip joint. It dropped free in his hand, only the pivot pin remained now to hold his leg on. He climbed slowly to his feet and moved towards Coleman's desk.

'Mr. Coleman, sir, it's time to go down to the ship now, should I leave now, sir?'

Jon spoke the words slowly as he walked forward, apparently going to the door, but angling at the same time towards the plump man's desk.

'You got thirty minutes yet, go sit – *say . . . !*'

The words were cut off. Fast as a human reflex is, it is the barest crawl compared to the lightning action of electronic reflex. At the instant Coleman was first aware of Jon's motion, the robot had finished his leap and lay sprawled across the desk, his leg off at the hip and clutched in his hand.

'*You'll kill yourself if you touch the button!*'

The words were part of the calculated plan. Jon bellowed them in the startled man's ear as he stuffed the dismembered leg down the front of the man's baggy slacks. It had the desired effect, Coleman's finger stabbed at the button but stopped before it made contact. He stared down with bulging eyes at the little black box of death peeping out of his waistband.

Jon hadn't waited for the reaction. He pushed backward from the desk and stopped to grab the stolen pinch bar off the floor. A mighty one-legged leap brought him to the locked closet; he stabbed the bar into the space between the door and frame and heaved.

Coleman was just starting to struggle the bomb out of his pants when the action was over. The closet open, Jon seized the heavy strap holding the second bomb on the rummy's chest and snapped it like a thread. He threw the bomb into Coleman's corner, giving the man one more thing to worry about. It had cost him a leg, but Jon had escaped the bomb threat without injuring a human. Now he had to get to a phone and make that call.

Coleman stopped tugging at the bomb and plunged his hand into the desk drawer for a gun. The returning men would block the door soon, the only other exit from the room was a frosted-glass window that opened onto the mammoth bay of the warehouse.

Jon Venex plunged through the window in a welter of flying glass. The heavy thud of a recoiless .75 came from the room behind him and a foot-long section of metal window frame leaped outward. Another slug screamed by the robot's head as he scrambled toward the rear door of the warehouse.

He was a bare thirty feet away from the back entrance when the giant door hissed shut on silent rollers. All the doors would have closed at the same time, the thud of running feet indicated that they would be guarded as well. Jon hopped a section of packing cases and crouched out of sight.

He looked up over his head, where there stretched a webbing of steel supports, crossing and recrossing until they joined the flat expanse of the roof. To human eyes the shadows there deepened into obscurity, but the infra-red from a network of steam pipes gave Jon all the illumination he needed.

The men would be quartering the floor of the warehouse soon, his only chance to escape recapture or death would be over their heads. Besides this, on the ground he was hampered by the loss of his leg. In the rafters he could use his arms for faster and easier travel.

Jon was just pulling himself up to one of the topmost cross beams when a hoarse shout from below was followed by a stream of bullets. They tore through the thin roof, one slug clanged off the steel beam under his body. Waiting until three of the newcomers had started up a nearby ladder, Jon began to quietly work his way towards the back of the building.

Safe for the moment, he took stock of his position. The men were spread out through the building, it could only be a matter of time before they found him. The doors were all locked and – he had made a complete circuit of the building to be sure – there were no windows that he could force. If he could call the emergency operator the unknown friends of Venex 17 might come to his aid. This, however, was out of the question. The only phone in the building was on Coleman's desk. He had traced the leads to make sure.

His eyes went automatically to the cables above his head. Plastic gaskets were set in the wall of the building, through them came the power and phone lines. The phone line! That was all he needed to make a call.

With smooth, fast motions he reached up and scratched a section of wire bare. He laughed to himself as he slipped the little microphone out of his left ear. Now he was half deaf as well as half lame – he was literally giving himself to this cause. He would have to remember the pun to tell Alec Diger later, if there was a later. Alec had a profound weakness for puns.

Jon attached jumpers to the mike and connected them to the bare wire. A touch of the ammeter showed that no one was on the line. He waited a few moments to be sure he had a dial tone then sent the eleven carefully spaced pulses that would connect him with the local operator. He placed the mike close to his mouth.

'Hello operator. Hello operator. I cannot hear you so do

not answer. Call the emergency operator – signal 14, I repeat – signal 14.'

Jon kept repeating the message until the searching men began to approach his position. He left the mike connected – the men wouldn't notice it in the dark but the open line would give the unknown powers his exact location. Using his fingertips he did a careful traverse on an *I* beam to an alcove in the farthest corner of the room. Escape was impossible, all he could do was stall for time.

'Mr. Coleman, I'm sorry I ran away.' With the volume on full his voice rolled like thunder from the echoing walls.

He could see the men below twisting their heads vainly to find the source.

'If you let me come back and don't kill me I will do your work. I was afraid of the bomb, but now I am afraid of the guns.' It sounded a little infantile, but he was pretty sure none of those present had any sound knowledge of robotic intelligence.

'Please let me come back ... sir!' He had almost forgotten the last word, so he added another 'Please, sir!' to make up.

Coleman needed that package under the boat very badly, he would promise anything to get it. Jon had no doubts as to his eventual fate, all he could hope to do was mark time in the hopes that the phone message would bring aid.

'Come on down, I won't be mad at you – if you follow directions.' Jon could hear the hidden anger in his voice, the unspoken hatred for a robe who dared lay hands on him.

The descent wasn't difficult, but Jon did it slowly with much apparent discomfort. He hopped into the center of the floor – leaning on the cases as if for support. Coleman and Druce were both there as well as a group of hard-eyed newcomers. They raised their guns at his approach but Coleman stopped them with a gesture.

'This is *my* robe boys, I'll see to it that he's happy.'

He raised his gun and shot Jon's remaining leg off. Twisted around by the blast Jon fell helplessly to the floor. He looked up into the smoking mouth of the .75.

'Very smart for a tin-can, but not smart enough. We'll get the junk on the boat some other way, some way that won't mean having you around under foot.' Death looked out of his narrowed eyes.

Less than two minutes had passed since Jon's call. The watchers must have been keeping 24-hour stations waiting for Venex 17's phone message.

The main door went down with the sudden scream of torn steel. A whippet tank crunched over the wreck and covered the group with its multiple pom-poms. They were an instant too late, Coleman pulled the trigger.

Jon saw the tensing trigger finger and pushed hard against the floor. His head rolled clear but the bullet tore through his shoulder. Coleman didn't have a chance for a second shot, there was a fizzling hiss from the tank and the riot ports released a flood of tear gas. The stricken men never saw the gas-masked police that poured in from the street.

Jon lay on the floor of the police station while a tech made temporary repairs on his leg and shoulder. Across the room Venex 17 was moving his new body with evident pleasure.

'Now this really feels like *something!* I was sure my time was up when that land slip caught me. But maybe I ought to start from the beginning.' He stamped across the room and shook Jon's inoperable hand.

'The name is Wil Counter-4951L3, not that *that* means much any more. I've worn so many different bodies that I forget what I originally looked like. I went right from factory-school to a police training school – and I have been on the job ever since – Force of Detectives, Sergeant Jr. grade, Investigation Department. I spend most of my time selling candy bars or newspapers, or serving drinks in crumb joints. Gather information, make reports and keep tab on guys for other departments.

'This last job – and I'm sorry I had to use a Venex identity, I don't think I brought any dishonor to your family – I was on loan to the Customs Department. Seems a ring was bringing uncut junk – heroin – into the country. F. B. I. tabbed all the operators here, but no one knew how the stuff got in. When Coleman, he's the local big-shot, called the agencies for an underwater robot, I was packed into a new body and sent running.

'I alerted the squad as soon as I started the tunnel, but the damned thing caved in on me before I found out what ship was doing the carrying. From there on you know what happened.

'Not knowing I was out of the game the squad sat tight and waited. The hop merchants saw a half million in snow sailing back to the old country so they had you dragged in as a replacement. You made the phone call and the cavalry rushed in at the last moment to save two robots from a rusty grave.'

Jon, who had been trying vainly to get in a word, saw his chance as Wil Counter turned to admire the reflection of his new figure in a window.

'You shouldn't be telling me those things – about your police investigations and department operations. Isn't this information supposed to be secret? Specially from robots!'

'Of course it is!' was Wil's airy answer. 'Captain Edge-combe – he's the head of my department – is an expert on all kinds of blackmail. I'm supposed to tell you so much confidential police business that you'll have to either join the department or be shot as a possible informer.' His laughter wasn't shared by the bewildered Jon.

'Truthfully Jon, we need you and can use you. Robes that can think fast and act fast aren't easy to find. After hearing about the tricks you pulled in that warehouse the Captain swore to decapitate me permanently if I couldn't get you to join up. Do you need a job? Long hours, short pay – but guaranteed to never get boring.'

Wil's voice was suddenly serious. 'You saved my life Jon – those snowbirds would have left me in that sandpile until all hell froze over. I'd like you for a mate, I think we could get along well together.' The gay note came back into his voice, 'And besides that, I may be able to save your life some day – I hate owing debts.'

The tech was finished, he snapped his tool box shut and left. Jon's shoulder motor was repaired now, he sat up. When they shook hands this time it was a firm clasp. The kind you know will last awhile.

Jon stayed in an empty cell that night. It was gigantic compared to the hotel and barrack rooms he was used to. He wished that he had his missing legs so he could take a little walk up and down the cell. He would have to wait until the morning. They were going to fix him up then before he started the new job.

He had recorded his testimony earlier and the impossible events of the past day kept whirling around in his head. He would think about it some other time, right now all he wanted to do was let his overworked circuits cool down, if he only had something to read, to focus his attention on. Then, with a start, he remembered the booklet. Everything had moved so fast that the earlier incident with the truckdriver had slipped his mind completely.

He carefully worked it out from behind the generator shielding and opened the first page of *Robot Slaves in a World Economy*. A card slipped from between the pages and he read the short message on it.

PLEASE DESTROY THIS CARD AFTER READING

If you think there is truth in this book and would like to hear more, come to Room B, 107 George St. any Tuesday at 5 P.M.

The card flared briefly and was gone. But he knew that it wasn't only a perfect memory that would make him remember that message.

There is no real reason why robots cannot be designed to do anything that a man might do. For those whose minds are constructed that way, and who think first of the male function when the word *man* is mentioned, it should be stated that parthenogenesis has already been induced mechanically in mammals. Nor should extra-uterine growth of fertilized ova in a suitable medium be beyond the scope of scientific achievement. Though artificial construction of the ovum itself, with the proper DNA chains, seems now to be so difficult as to border on the verge of impossibility.

Mankind can still perform these functions adequately and pleasurably, without any outside aid. But there are numbers of other jobs that men do that they would be only too willing to turn over to the robots. No one really sets out in life with the ambition to be a garbage collector, though this is an important and essential function of civilization. Proof of this position's lack of desirability can be seen by the fact that it is always the poorest and most under-privileged groups who staff the lower ranks of the department of sanitation. A look at your garbageman will quickly tell you which social group is at the bottom of the pecking order in your community.

Undoubtedly robots will be garbagemen and boiler cleaners, physical laborers and harvest hands. They will also fill the more hazardous positions. Underwater obstacles will be removed from swift-flowing channels by them, and they will repair atomic generators in radioactive rooms that would be instant death to a human being.

They might also have a function in law enforcement....

ARM OF THE LAW

It was a big, coffin-shaped plywood box that looked like it weighed a ton. This brawny type just dumped it through the door of the police station and started away. I looked up from the blotter and shouted at the trucker's vanishing back.

'What the hell is that?'

'How should I know,' he said as he swung up into the cab. 'I just deliver, I don't X-ray, 'em. It came on the morning rocket from earth is all I know.' He gunned the truck more than he had to and threw up a billowing cloud of red dust.

'Jokers,' I growled to myself. 'Mars is full of jokers.'

When I went over to look at the box I could feel the dust grate between my teeth. Chief Craig must have heard the racket because he came out of his office and helped me stand and look at the box.

'Think it's a bomb?' he asked in a bored voice.

'Why would anyone bother – particularly with a thing this size? And all the way from earth.'

He nodded agreement and walked around to look at the other end. There was no sender's address anywhere on the outside. Finally we had to dig out the crowbar and I went to work on the top. After some prying it pulled free and fell off.

That was when we had our first look at Ned. We all would have been a lot happier if it had been our last look as well. If we had just put the lid back on and shipped the thing back to earth! I know now what they mean about Pandora's Box.

But we just stood there and stared like a couple of rubes.

Ned lay motionless and stared back at us.

'A robot!' the Chief said.

'Very observant; it's easy to see you went to the police academy.'

'Ha ha! Now find out what he's doing here.'

I hadn't gone to the academy, but this was no handicap to my finding the letter. It was sticking up out of a thick book in a pocket in the box. The Chief took the letter and read it with little enthusiasm.

'Well, well! United Robotics have the brainstorm that ... *robots, correctly used, will tend to prove invaluable in police work* ... they want us to co-operate in a field test ... *robot enclosed is the latest experimental model; valued at 120,000 credits.*'

We both looked back at the robot, sharing the wish that the credits had been in the box instead of it. The Chief frowned and moved his lips through the rest of the letter. I wondered how we got the robot out of its plywood coffin.

Experimental model or not, this was a nice-looking hunk of machinery. A uniform navy-blue all over, though the outlet cases, hooks and such were a metallic gold. Someone had gone to a lot of trouble to get that effect. This was as close as a robot could look to a cop in uniform, without being a joke. All that seemed to be missing was the badge and gun.

Then I noticed the tiny glow of light in the robot's eye lenses. It had never occurred to me before that the thing might be turned on. There was nothing to lose by finding out.

'Get out of that box,' I said.

The robot came up smooth and fast as a rocket, landing two feet in front of me and whipping out a snappy salute.

'Police Experimental Robot, serial number XPO–456–934B reporting for duty, sir.'

His voice quivered with alertness and I could almost hear the humming of those taut cable muscles. He may have had a stainless steel hide and a bunch of wires for a brain – but he spelled rookie cop to me just the same. The fact that he was man-height with two arms, two legs and that painted-on uniform helped. All I had to do was squint my eyes a bit and there stood Ned the Rookie Cop. Fresh out of school and raring to go. I shook my head to get rid of the illusion. This was just six feet of machine that boffins and brain-boys had turned out for their own amusement.

'Relax, Ned,' I said. He was still holding the salute. 'At ease. You'll get a hernia of your exhaust pipe if you stay so tense. Anyways, I'm just the sergeant here. That's the Chief of Police over there.'

Ned did an about face and slid over to the Chief with that same greased-lightning motion. The Chief just looked at him like something that sprang out from under the hood of a car, while Ned went through the same report routine.

'I wonder if it does anything else beside salute and report,' the Chief said while he walked around the robot, looking it over like a dog with a hydrant.

'The functions, operations and responsible courses of action open to the Police Experimental Robots are outlined on pages 184 to 213 of the manual.' Ned's voice was muffled for a second while he half-dived back into his case and came up with the volume mentioned. 'A detailed breakdown of these will also be found on pages 1035 to 1267 inclusive.'

The Chief, who has trouble reading an entire comic page at one sitting, turned the 6-inch thick book over in his hands like it would maybe bite him. When he had a rough idea of how much it weighed and a good feel of the binding he threw it on my desk.

'Take care of this,' he said to me as he headed towards his office. 'And the robot too. Do something with it.' The Chief's span of attention never was great and it had been strained to the limit this time.

I flipped through the book, wondering. One thing I never have had much to do with is robots, so I know just as much about them as any Joe in the street. Probably less. The book was filled with pages of fine print, fancy mathematics, wiring diagrams and charts in nine colors and that kind of thing. It needed close attention. Which attention I was not prepared to give at the time. The book slid shut and I eyed the newest employee of the city of Nineport.

'There is a broom behind the door. Do you know how to use it?'

'Yes, sir.'

'In that case you will sweep out this room, raising as small a cloud of dust as possible at the same time.'

He did a very neat job of it.

I watched 120,000 credits' worth of machinery making a tidy pile of butts and sand and wondered why it had been sent to Nineport. Probably because there wasn't another police force in the solar system that was smaller or more unimportant than ours. The engineers must have figured this would be a good spot for a field test. Even if the thing blew up, nobody would really mind. There would probably be someone along some day to get a report on it. Well, they had picked the right spot all right. Nineport was just a little bit beyond nowhere.

Which, of course, was why I was there. I was the only real cop on the force. They needed at least one to give an illusion of the wheels going around. The Chief, Alonzo Craig, had just enough sense to take graft without dropping the money. There were two patrolmen. One old and drunk most of the time. The other so young he still had diaper rash. I had ten years on a metropolitan force, earthside. Why I left is nobody's damn business. I have long since paid for any mistakes I made there by ending up in Nineport.

Nineport is not a city, it's just a place where people stop. The only permanent citizens are the ones who cater to those on the way through. Hotel keepers, gamblers, whores, barkeeps, and the rest.

There is a spaceport, but only some freighters come there. To pick up the metal from some of the mines that are still working. Some of the settlers still come in for supplies. You might say that Nineport was a town that just missed the boat. In a hundred years I doubt if there will be enough left sticking out of the sand to even tell where it used to be.

I won't be there either, so I couldn't care less.

I went back to the blotter. Five drunks in the tank, an average night's haul. While I wrote them up Fats dragged in the sixth one.

'Locked himself in the ladies' john at the spaceport and resisting arrest,' he reported.

'D and D. Throw him in with the rest.'

Fats steered his limp victim across the floor, matching him step for dragging step. I always marveled at the way Fats took care of drunks, since he usually had more under his belt than they had. I have never seen him falling down drunk or completely sober. About all he was good for was keeping a blurred eye on the lockup and running in drunks. He did well at that. No matter what they crawled under or on top of, he found them. No doubt due to the same shared natural instincts.

Fats clanged the door behind number six and weaved his way back in. 'What's that?' he asked, peering at the robot along the purple beauty of his nose.

'That is a robot. I have forgotten the number his mother gave him at the factory so we will call him Ned. He works here now.'

'Good for him! He can clean up the tank after we throw the bums out.'

'That's *my* job,' Billy said coming in through the front door. He clutched his nightstick and scowled out from under the brim of his uniform cap. It is not that Billy is stupid, just that most of his strength has gone into his back instead of his mind.

'That's Ned's job now because you have a promotion. You are going to help me with some of my work.'

Billy came in very handy at times and I was anxious that the force shouldn't lose him. My explanation cheered him because he sat down by Fats and watched Ned do the floor.

That's the way things went for about a week. We watched Ned sweep and polish until the station began to take on a positively antiseptic look. The Chief, who always has an eye out for that type of thing, found out that Ned

could file the odd ton of reports and paperwork that clut-
tered his office. All this kept the robot busy, and we got so
used to him we were hardly aware he was around. I knew
he had moved the packing case into the storeroom and fixed
himself up a cozy sort of robot dormitory-coffin. Other than
that I didn't know or care.

The operation manual was buried in my desk and I never
looked at it. If I had, I might have had some idea of the big
changes that were in store. None of us knew the littlest bit
about what a robot can or cannot do. Ned was working
nicely as a combination janitor-fileclerk and should have
stayed that way. He would have too if the Chief hadn't been
so lazy. That's what started it all.

It was around nine at night and the Chief was just going
home when the call came in. He took it, listened for a
moment, then hung up.

'Greenback's liquor store. He got held up again. Says to
come at once.'

'That's a change. Usually we don't hear about it until a
month later. What's he paying protection money for if
China Joe ain't protecting? What's the rush now?'

The Chief chewed his loose lip for awhile, finally and
painfully reached a decision.

'You better go around and see what the trouble is.'

'Sure,' I said reaching for my cap. 'But no one else is
around, you'll have to watch the desk until I get back.'

'That's no good,' he moaned. 'I'm dying from hunger and
sitting here isn't going to help me any.'

'I will go take the report,' Ned said, stepping forward and
snapping his usual well-greased salute.

At first the Chief wasn't buying. You would think the
water cooler came to life and offered to take over his job.

'How could *you* take a report?' he growled, putting the
wise-guy water cooler in its place. But he had phrased his
little insult as a question so he had only himself to blame.
In exactly three minutes Ned gave the Chief a summary of
the routine necessary for a police officer to make a report
on an armed robbery or other reported theft. From the

glazed look in the Chief's protruding eyes I could tell Ned had quickly passed the boundaries of the Chief's meager knowledge.

'Enough!' the harried man finally gasped. 'If you know so much why don't you make a report?'

Which to me sounded like another version of '*if you're so damned smart why ain't you rich?*' which we used to snarl at the brainy kids in grammar school. Ned took such things literally though, and turned towards the door.

'Do you mean you wish me to make a report on this robbery?'

'Yes,' the Chief said just to get rid of him, and we watched his blue shape vanish through the door.

'He must be brighter than he looks,' I said. 'He never stopped to ask where Greenback's store is.'

The Chief nodded and the phone rang again. His hand was still resting on it so he picked it up by reflex. He listened for a second and you would have thought someone was pumping blood out of his heel from the way his face turned white.

'The holdup's still on,' he finally gasped. 'Greenback's delivery boy is on the line – calling back to see where we are. Says he's under a table in the back room....'

I never heard the rest of it because I was out the door and into the car. There were a hundred things that could happen if Ned got there before me. Guns could go off, people hurt, lots of things. And the police would be to blame for it all – sending a tin robot to do a cop's job. Maybe the Chief had ordered Ned there, but clearly as if the words were painted on the windshield of the car, I knew I would be dragged into it. It never gets very warm on Mars, but I was sweating.

Nineport has fourteen traffic regulations and I broke all of them before I had gone a block. Fast as I was, Ned was faster. As I turned the corner I saw him open the door of Greenback's store and walk in. I screamed brakes in behind him and arrived just in time to have a gallery seat. A shooting gallery at that.

There were two holdup punks, one behind the counter making like a clerk and the other lounging off to the side. Their guns were out of sight, but blue-coated Ned busting through the door like that was too much for their keyed-up nerves. Up came both guns like they were on strings and Ned stopped dead. I grabbed for my own gun and waited for pieces of busted robot to come flying through the window.

Ned's reflexes were great. Which I suppose is what you should expect of a robot.

'DROP YOUR GUNS, YOU ARE UNDER ARREST.'

He must have had on full power or something, his voice blasted so loud my ears hurt. The result was just what you might expect. Both torpedoes let go at once and the air was filled with flying slugs. The show windows went out with a crash and I went down on my stomach. From the amount of noise I knew they both had recoilless .50's. You can't stop one of those slugs. They go right through you and anything else that happens to be in the way.

Except they didn't seem to be bothering Ned. The only notice he seemed to take was to cover his eyes. A little shield with a thin slit popped down over his eye lenses. Then he moved in on the first thug.

I knew he was fast, but not that fast. A couple of slugs jarred him as he came across the room, but before the punk could change his aim Ned had the gun in his hand. That was the end of that. He put on one of the sweetest hammer locks I have ever seen and neatly grabbed the gun when it dropped from the limp fingers. With the same motion that slipped the gun into a pouch he whipped out a pair of handcuffs and snapped them on the punk's wrists.

Holdupnik number two was heading for the door by then, and I was waiting to give him a warm reception. There was never any need. He hadn't gone halfway before Ned slid in front of him. There was a thud when they hit that didn't even shake Ned, but gave the other a glazed look. He never even knew it when Ned slipped the cuffs on him and dropped him down next to his partner.

I went in, took their guns from Ned, and made the arrest
official. That was all Greenback saw when he crawled out
from behind the counter and it was all I wanted him to see.
The place was a foot deep in broken glass and smelled like
the inside of a Jack Daniels bottle. Greenback began to
howl like a wolf over his lost stock. He didn't seem to know
any more about the phone call than I did, so I grabbed
ahold of a pimply-looking kid who staggered out of the
storeroom. He was the one who had made the calls.

It turned out to be a matter of sheer stupidity. He had
worked for Greenback only a few days and didn't have
enough brains to realize that all holdups should be reported
to the protection boys instead of the police. I told Greenback to wise up his boy, as look at the trouble that got
caused. Then pushed the two ex-holdup men out to the car.
Ned climbed in back with them and they clung together like
two waifs in a storm. The robot's only response was to pull
a first aid kit from his hip and fix up a ricochet hole in one
of the thugs that no one had noticed in the excitement.

The Chief was still sitting there with that bloodless look
when we marched in. I didn't believe it could be done, but
he went two shades whiter.

'You made the pinch,' he whispered. Before I could
straighten him out a second and more awful idea hit him.
He grabbed a handful of shirt on the first torpedo and
poked his face down. 'You with China Joe,' he snarled.

The punk made the error of trying to be cute so the
Chief let him have one on the head with the open hand that
set his eyes rolling like marbles. When the question got
asked again he found the right answer.

'I never heard from no China Joe. We just hit town today
and—'

'Freelance, by God,' the Chief sighed and collapsed into
his chair. 'Lock 'em up and quickly tell me what in hell
happened.'

I slammed the gate on them and pointed a none too
steady finger at Ned.

'There's the hero,' I said. 'Took them on single-handed,

rassled them for a fall and made the capture. He is a one-robot tornado, a power for good in this otherwise evil community. And he's bullet-proof too.' I ran a finger over Ned's broad chest. The paint was chipped by the slugs, but the metal was hardly scratched.

'This is going to cause me trouble, big trouble,' the Chief wailed.

I knew he meant with the protection boys. They did not like punks getting arrested and guns going off without their okay. But Ned thought the Chief had other worries and rushed in to put them right. 'There will be no trouble. At no time did I violate any of the Robotic Restriction Laws, they are part of my control circuits and therefore fully automatic. The men who drew their guns violated both robotic and human law when they threatened violence. I did not injure the men – merely restrained them.'

It was all over the Chief's head, but I liked to think *I* could follow it. And I *had* been wondering how a robot – a machine – could be involved in something like law application and violence. Ned had the answer to that one too.

'Robots have been assuming these functions for years. Don't recording radar meters pass judgment on human violation of automobile regulations? A robot alcohol detector is better qualified to assess the sobriety of a prisoner than the arresting officer. At one time robots were even allowed to make their own decisions about killing. Before the Robotic Restriction Laws automatic gun-pointers were in general use. Their final development was a self-contained battery of large anti-aircraft guns. Automatic scan radar detected all aircraft in the vicinity. Those that could not return the correct identifying signal had their courses tracked and computed, automatic fuse-cutters and loaders readied the computer-aimed guns – which were fired by the robot mechanism.'

There was little I could argue about with Ned. Except maybe his college-professor vocabulary. So I switched the attack.

'But a robot can't take the place of a cop, it's a complex human job.'

'Of course it is, but taking a human policeman's place is not the function of a police robot. Primarily I combine the functions of numerous pieces of police equipment, integrating their operations and making them instantly available. In addition I can aid in the *mechanical* processes of law enforcement. If you arrest a man you handcuff him. But if you order me to do it, I have made no moral decision. I am just a machine for attaching handcuffs at that point. . . .'

My raised hand cut off the flow of robotic argument. Ned was hipped to his ears with facts and figures and I had a good idea who would come off second best in any continued discussion. No laws had been broken when Ned made the pinch, that was for sure. But there are other laws than those that appear on the books.

'China Joe is not going to like this, not at all,' the Chief said, speaking my own thoughts.

The law of Tooth and Claw. That's one that wasn't in the law books. And that was what ran Nineport. The place was just big enough to have a good population of gambling joints, bawdy houses and drunk-rollers. They were all run by China Joe. As was the police department. We were all in his pocket and you might say he was the one who paid our wages. This is not the kind of thing, though, that you explain to a robot.

'Yeah, China Joe.'

I thought it was an echo at first, then realized that someone had eased in the door behind me. Something called Alex. Six feet of bone, muscle and trouble. China Joe's right-hand man. He imitated a smile at the Chief who sank a bit lower in his chair.

'China Joe wants you should tell him why you got smart cops going around and putting the arm on people and letting them shoot up good liquor. He's mostly angry about the hooch. He says that he had enough guff and after this you should—'

'I am putting you under Robot Arrest, pursuant to article

46, paragraph 19 of the revised statutes....'

Ned had done it before we realized he had even moved. Right in front of our eyes he was arresting Alex and signing our death warrants.

Alex was not slow. As he turned to see who had grabbed him, he had already dragged out his cannon. He got one shot in, square against Ned's chest, before the robot plucked the gun away and slipped on the cuffs. While we all gaped like dead fish, Ned recited the charge in what I swear was a satisfied tone.

'The prisoner is Peter Rakjomskj, alias Alex the Axe, wanted in Canal City for armed robbery and attempted murder. Also wanted by local police of Detroit, New York and Manchester on charges of....'

'Get it off me!' Alex howled. We might have too, and everything might have still been straightened out if Benny Bug hadn't heard the shot. He popped his head in the front door just long enough to roll his eyes over our little scene.

'Alex ... they're puttin' the arm on Alex!'

Then he was gone and when I hit the door he was nowhere in sight. China Joe's boys always went around in pairs. And in ten minutes he would know all about it.

'Book him,' I told Ned. 'It wouldn't make any difference if we let him go now. The world has already come to an end.'

Fats came in then, mumbling to himself. He jerked a thumb over his shoulder when he saw me.

'What's up? I see little Benny Bug come out of here like the place was on fire and almost get killed driving away?'

Then Fats saw Alex with the bracelets on and turned sober in one second. He just took a moment to gape, then his mind was made up. Without a trace of a stagger he walked over to the Chief and threw his badge on the desk in front of him.

'I am an old man and I drink too much to be a cop. Therefore I am resigning from the force. Because if that is whom I think it is over there with the cuffs on, I will not live to be a day older as long as I am around here.'

'Rat.' The Chief growled in pain through his clenched teeth. 'Deserting the sinking ship. Rat.'

'Squeak,' Fats said and left.

The Chief was beyond caring at this point. He didn't blink an eye when I took Fats' badge off the desk. I don't know why I did it, perhaps I thought it was only fair. Ned had started all the trouble and I was just angry enough to want him on the spot when it was finished. There were two rings on his chest plate, and I was not surprised when the badge pin fitted them neatly.

'There, now you are a real cop.' Sarcasm dripped from the words. I should have realized that robots are immune to sarcasm. Ned took my statement at face value.

'This is a very great honor, not only for me but for all robots. I will do my best to fulfill all the obligations of the office.' Jack Armstrong in tin underwear. I could hear the little motors in his guts humming with joy as he booked Alex.

If everything else hadn't been so bad I would have enjoyed that. Ned had more police equipment built into him than Nineport had ever owned. There was an ink pad that snapped out of one hip, and he efficiently rolled Alex's fingertips across it and stamped them on a card. Then he held the prisoner at arm's length while something clicked in his abdomen. Once more sideways and two instant photographs dropped out of a slot. The mug shots were stuck on the card, arrest details and such inserted. There was more like this, but I forced myself away. There were more important things to think about.

Like staying alive.

'Any ideas Chief?'

A groan was my only answer so I let it go at that. Billy, the balance of the police force, came in then. I gave him a quick rundown. Either through stupidity or guts he elected to stay, and I was proud of the boy. Ned locked away the latest prisoner and began sweeping up.

That was the way we were when China Joe walked in.

Even though we were expecting it, it was still a shock. He

had a bunch of his toughest hoods with him and they crowded through the door like an overweight baseball team. China Joe was in front, hands buried in the sleeves of his long mandarin gown. No expression at all on his Asiatic features. He didn't waste time talking to us, just gave the word to his own boys.

'Clean this place up. The new police Chief will be here in a while and I don't want him to see any bums hanging around.'

It made me angry. Even with the graft I like to feel I'm still a cop. Not on a cheap punk's payroll. I was also curious about China Joe. Had been ever since I tried to get a line on him and never found a thing. I still wanted to know.

'Ned, take a good look at that Chinese guy in the rayon bathrobe and let me know who he is.'

My, but those electronic circuits work fast. Ned shot the answer back like a straight man who had been rehearsing his lines for weeks.

'He is a pseudo-oriental, utilizing a natural sallowness of the skin heightened with dye. He is not Chinese. There has also been an operation on his eyes, scars of which are still visible. This has been undoubtedly done in an attempt to conceal his real identity, but Bertillon measurements of his ears and other features make identity positive. He is on the Very Wanted list of Interpol and his real name is . . .'

China Joe was angry, and with a reason.

'That's the *thing* . . . that big-mouthed tin radio set over there. We heard about it and we're taking care of it!'

The mob jumped aside then or hit the deck and I saw there was a guy kneeling in the door with a rocket launcher. Shaped anti-tank charges, no doubt. That was my last thought as the thing let go with a 'whoosh.'

Maybe you can hit a tank with one of those. But not a robot. At least not a police robot. Ned was sliding across the floor on his face when the back wall blew up. There was no second shot. Ned closed his hand on the tube of the bazooka and it was so much old drainpipe.

Billy decided then that anyone who fired a rocket in a
police station was breaking the law, so he moved in with
his club. I was right behind him since I did not want to
miss any of the fun. Ned was at the bottom somewhere, but
I didn't doubt he could take care of himself.

There were a couple of muffled shots and someone
screamed. No one fired after that because we were too
tangled up. A punk named Brooklyn Eddie hit me on the
side of the head with his gunbutt and I broke his nose all
over his face with my fist.

There is a kind of a fog over everything after that. But I
do remember it was very busy for awhile.

When the fog lifted a bit I realized I was the only one
still standing. Or leaning rather. It was a good thing the
wall was there.

Ned came in through the street door carrying a very
bashed looking Brooklyn Eddie. I hoped I had done all
that. Eddie's wrists were fastened together with cuffs. Ned
laid him gently next to the heap of thugs – who I suddenly
realized all wore the same kind of handcuffs. I wondered
vaguely if Ned made them as he needed them or had a
supply tucked away in a hollow leg or something.

There was a chair a few feet away and sitting down
helped.

Blood was all over everything and if a couple of the
hoods hadn't groaned I would have thought they were
corpses. One was, I noticed suddenly. A bullet had caught
him in the chest, most of the blood was probably his.

Ned burrowed in the bodies for a moment and dragged
Billy out. He was unconscious. A big smile on his face and
the splintered remains of his nightstick still stuck in his fist.
It takes very little to make some people happy. A bullet
had gone through his leg and he never moved while Ned
ripped the pants leg off and put on a bandage.

'The spurious China Joe and one other man escaped in a
car,' Ned reported.

'Don't let it worry you,' I managed to croak. 'Your batting average still leads the league.'

It was then I realized the Chief was still sitting in his chair, where he had been when the bruhaha started. Still slumped down with that glazed look. Only after I started to talk to him did I realize that Alonzo Craig, Chief of Police of Nineport, was now dead.

A single shot. Small caliber gun, maybe a .22. Right through the heart and what blood there had been was soaked up by his clothes. I had a good idea where the gun would be that fired that shot. A small gun, the kind that would fit in a wide Chinese sleeve.

I wasn't tired or groggy any more. Just angry. Maybe he hadn't been the brightest or most honest guy in the world. But he deserved a better end than that. Knocked off by a two-bit racket boss who thought he was being crossed.

Right about then I realized I had a big decision to make. With Billy out of the fight and Fats gone I was the Nineport police force. All I had to do to be clear of this mess was to walk out the door and keep going. I would be safe enough.

Ned buzzed by, picked up two of the thugs, and hauled them off to the cells.

Maybe it was the sight of his blue back or maybe I was tired of running. Either way my mind was made up before I realized it. I carefully took off the Chief's gold badge and put it on in place of my old one.

'The new Chief of Police of Nineport,' I said to no one in particular.

'Yes, sir,' Ned said as he passed. He put one of the prisoners down long enough to salute, then went on with his work. I returned the salute.

The hospital meat wagon hauled away the dead and wounded. I took an evil pleasure in ignoring the questioning stares of the attendants. After the doc fixed the side of my head, everyone cleared out. Ned mopped up the floor. I ate ten aspirin and waited for the hammering to stop so I could think what to do next.

When I pulled my thoughts together the answer was

obvious. Too obvious. I made as long a job as I could of
reloading my gun.

'Refill your handcuff box, Ned. We are going out.'

Like a good cop he asked no questions. I locked the outside door when we left and gave him the key.

'Here. There's a good chance you will be the only one left
to use this before the day is over.'

I stretched the drive over to China Joe's place just as
much as I could. Trying to figure if there was another way
of doing it. There wasn't. Murder had been done and Joe
was the boy I was going to pin it on. So I had to get him.

The best I could do was stop around the corner and give
Ned a briefing.

'This combination bar and hookshop is the sole property
of he whom we will still call China Joe until there is time
for you to give me a rundown on him. Right now I got
enough distractions. What we have to do is go in there, find
Joe and bring him to justice. Simple?'

'Simple,' Ned answered in his sharp Joe-college voice.
'But wouldn't it be simple to make the arrest now, when he
is leaving in that car, instead of waiting until he returns?'

The car in mention was doing sixty as it came out of the
alley ahead of us. I only had a glimpse of Joe in the back
seat as it tore by us.

'Stop them!' I shouted, mostly for my own benefit since I
was driving. I tried to shift gears and start the engine at the
same time, and succeeded in doing exactly nothing.

So Ned stopped them. It had been phrased as an order.
He leaned his head out of the window and I saw at once
why most of his equipment was located in his torso. Probably his brain as well. There sure wasn't much room left in
his head when that cannon was tucked away in there.

A .75 recoilless. A plate swiveled back right where his
nose should have been if he had one, and the big muzzle
pointed out. It's a neat idea when you think about it. Right
between the eyes for good aiming, up high, always ready.

The BOOM BOOM almost took my head off. Of course
Ned was a perfect shot – so would I be with a computer for

a brain. He had holed one rear tire with each slug and the car flap-flapped to a stop a little ways down the road. I climbed out slowly while Ned sprinted there in seconds flat. They didn't even try to run this time. What little nerve they had left must have been shattered by the smoking muzzle of that .75 poking out from between Ned's eyes. Robots are neat about things like that so he must have left it sticking out deliberate. Probably had a course in psychology back in robot school.

Three of them in the car, all waving their hands in the air like the last reel of a western. And the rear floor covered with interesting little suitcases.

Everyone came along quietly.

China Joe only snarled while Ned told me that his name really was Stantin and the Elmira hot seat was kept warm all the time in hopes he would be back. I promised Joe-Stantin I would be happy to arrange it that same day. Thereby not worrying about any slip-ups with the local authorities. The rest of the mob would stand trial in Canal City.

It was a very busy day.

Things have quieted down a good deal since then. Billy is out of the hospital and wearing my old sergeant's stripes. Even Fats is back, though he is sober once in a while now and has trouble looking me in the eye. We don't have much to do because in addition to being a quiet town this is now an honest one.

Ned is on foot patrol nights and in charge of the lab and files days. Maybe the Policeman's Benevolent wouldn't like that, but Ned doesn't seem to mind. He touched up all the bullet scratches and keeps his badge polished. I know a robot can't be happy or sad – but Ned *seems* to be happy.

Sometimes I would swear I can hear him humming to himself. But, of course that is only the motors and things going around.

When you start thinking about it, I suppose we set some kind of precedent here. What with putting on a robot as a full-fledged police officer. No one ever came around from the factory yet, so I have never found out if we're the first or not.

And I'll tell you something else. I'm not going to stay in this broken-down town forever. I have some letters out now, looking for a new job.

So some people are going to be *very* surprised when they see who their new Chief of Police is after *I* leave.

Like human slaves or serfs, robots will not need – from the point of view of their masters, anyway – any unnecessary education. A serf 'needs' to know only such information as relates to farming, and how to do what he's told – fast. Anything more is pointless, and potentially dangerous, since it tends to raise such nasty questions as, Is this the way it should be? And next thing you know, faithful Wamba is studying out ways to burn down the manor house and sharpening his sickle meaningfully.... It's too soon to *know* if robots would react the same way, but they, too, will only 'know' what they have to – expense alone would see to that.

Yet some robots will have to have access to information that they have no immediate need for. For example, a robot librarian would need a well-stocked memory just to answer a simple question....

THE ROBOT WHO WANTED TO KNOW

That was the trouble with Filer 13B-445-K, he wanted to know things that he had just no business knowing. Things that *no* robot should be interested in – much less investigate. But Filer was a very different type of robot.

The trouble with the blonde in tier 22 should have been warning enough for him. He had hummed out of the stack room with a load of books, and was cutting through tier 22 when he saw her bending over for a volume on the bottom shelf.

As he passed behind her he slowed down, then stopped a few yards further on. He watched her intently, a strange glint in his metallic eyes.

As the girl bent over her short skirt rode up to display an astonishing length of nylon-clad leg. That it was a singularly attractive leg should have been of no interest to a robot – yet it was. He stood there, looking, until the blonde turned suddenly and noticed his fixed attention.

'If you were human, Buster,' she said, 'I would slap your face. But since you are a robot, I would like to know what your little photon-filled eyes find so interesting?'

Without a microsecond's hesitation, Filer answered, 'Your seam is crooked.' Then he turned and buzzed away.

The blonde shook her head in wonder, straightened the offending stocking, and chalked up another credit to the honor of electronics.

She would have been very surprised to find out what Filer had been looking at. He *had* been staring at her leg. Of course he hadn't lied when he answered her – since he was incapable of lying – but he had been looking at a lot more than the crooked seam. Filer was facing a problem that no other robot had ever faced before.

Love, romance, and sex were fast becoming a passionate interest for him.

That this interest was purely academic goes without saying, yet it was still an interest. It was the nature of his work that first aroused his curiosity about the realm of Venus.

A Filer is an amazingly intelligent robot and there aren't very many being manufactured. You will find them only in the greatest libraries, dealing with only the largest and most complex collections. To call them simply librarians is to demean all librarians and to call their work simple. Of course very little intelligence is required to shelf books or stamp cards, but this sort of work has long been handled by robots that are little more than wheeled IBM machines. The cataloging of human information has always been an incredibly complex task. The Filer robots were the ones who finally inherited this job. It rested easier on their metallic shoulders than it ever had on the rounded ones of human librarians.

Besides a complete memory, Filer had other attributes that are usually connected with the human brain. Abstract connections for one thing. If he was asked for books on one subject, he could think of related books in other subjects that might be referred to. He could take a suggestion, pyramid it into a category, then produce tactile results in the form of a mountain of books.

These traits are usually confined to homo sapiens. They are the things that pulled him that last, long step above his animal relatives. If Filer was more than other robots, he had only his builders to blame.

He blamed no one – he was just interested. All Filers are interested, they are designed that way. Another Filer, 9B-367-O, librarian at the university in Tashkent, had turned his interest to language due to the immense amount of material at his disposal. He spoke thousands of languages and dialects, all that he could find texts on, and enjoyed a fine reputation in linguistic circles. That was because of his library. Filer 13B, he of the interest in girls' legs, labored in the dust-filled corridors of New Washington. In addition to all the gleaming new microfiles, he had access to tons of ancient printed-on-paper books that dated back for centuries.

Filer had found *his* interest in the novels of that by-gone time.

At first he was confused by all the references to *love* and *romance*, as well as the mental and physical suffering that seemed to accompany them. He could find no satisfactory or complete definition of the terms and was intrigued. Intrigue led to interest and finally absorption. Unknown to the world at large, he became an authority on Love.

Very early in his interest, Filer realized that this was the most delicate of all human institutions. He therefore kept his researches a secret and the only records he had were in the capacious circuits of his brain. Just about the same time he discovered that he could do research *in vivo* to supplement the facts in his books. This happened when he found a couple locked in embrace in the zoology section.

Quickly stepping back into the shadows, Filer had turned up the gain on his audio pickup. The resulting dialogue he heard was dull to say the least. A grey and wasted shadow of the love lyrics he knew from his books. This comparison was interesting and enlightening.

After that he listened to male–female conversations whenever he had the opportunity. He also tried to look at women from the viewpoint of men, and vice versa. This is what had led him to the lower-limb observation in tier 22.

It also led him to his ultimate folly.

A researcher sought his aid a few weeks later and fumbled out a thick pile of reference notes. A card slid from the notes and fell unnoticed to the floor. Filer picked it up and handed it back to the man who put it away with mumbled thanks. After the man had been supplied with the needed books and gone, Filer sat back and reread the card. He had only seen it for a split second, and upside down at that, but that was all he needed. The image of the card was imprinted forever in his brain. Filer mused over the card and the first glimmerings of an idea assailed him.

The card had been an invitation to a masquerade ball. He was well acquainted with this type of entertainment – it was stock-in-trade for his dusty novels. People went to them disguised as various romantic figures.

Why couldn't a robot go, disguised as people?

Once the idea was fixed in his head there was no driving it out. It was an un-robot thought and a completely un-robot action. Filer had a glimmering for the first time that he was breaking down the barrier between himself and the mysteries of romance. This only made him more eager to go. And of course he did.

Of course he didn't dare purchase a costume, but there was no problem in obtaining some ancient curtains from one of the storerooms. A book on sewing taught him the technique and a plate from a book gave him the design for his costume. It was predestined that he go as a cavalier.

With a finely ground pen point he printed an exact duplicate of the invitation on heavy card stock. His mask was part face and part mask, it offered no barrier to his talent or technology. Long before the appointed date he was ready. The last days were filled with browsing through stories about other masquerade balls and learning the latest dance steps.

So enthused was he by the idea that he never stopped to ponder the strangeness of what he was doing. He was just a scientist studying a species of animal. Man. Or rather woman.

The night finally arrived and he left the library late with what looked like a package of books and of course wasn't. No one noticed him enter the patch of trees on the library grounds. If they had, they would certainly never have connected him with the elegant gentleman who swept out of the far side a few moments later. Only the empty wrapping paper bore mute evidence of the disguise.

Filer's manner in his new personality was all that might be expected of a superior robot who has studied a role to

perfection. He swept up the stairs to the hall, three at a
time, and tendered his invitation with a flourish. Once inside he headed straight for the bar and threw down three
glasses of champagne, right through a plastic tube to a tank
in his thorax. Only then did he let his eye roam over the
assembled beauties. It was a night for love.

And of all the women in the room, there was only one he
had eyes for. Filer could see instantly that she was the belle
of the ball and the only one to approach. Could he do anything else in memory of 50,000 heroes of those long-for-
gotten books?

Carol Ann van Damm was bored as usual. Her face was
disguised, but no mask could hide the generous contours of
her bosom and flanks. All her usual suitors were there,
dancing attendance behind their dominoes, lusting after her
youth and her father's money. It was all too familiar and
she had trouble holding back her yawns.

Until the pack was courteously but irrevocably pushed
aside by the wide shoulders of the stranger. He was a lion
among wolves as he swept through them and faced her.

'This *is* our dance,' he said in a deep voice rich with
meaning. Almost automatically she took the proferred
hand, unable to resist this man with the strange gleam in
his eyes. In a moment they were waltzing and it was
heaven. His muscles were like steel yet he was light and
graceful as a god.

'Who are you?' she whispered.

'Your prince, come to take you away from all this,' he
murmured in her ear.

'You talk like a fairy tale,' she laughed.

'This is a fairy tale, and you are the heroine.'

His words struck fire from her brain and she felt the thrill
of an electric current sweep through her. It had, just a temporary short circuit. While his lips murmured the words she
had wanted to hear all her life into her ear, his magic feet
led her though the great doors onto the balcony. Once there
words blended with action and hot lips burned against hers.

102 degrees to be exact, that was what the thermostat was set at.

'Please,' she breathed, weak with this new passion, 'I must sit down.' He sat next to her, her hands in his soft yet vise-like grip. They talked the words that only lovers know until a burst of music drew her attention.

'Midnight,' she breathed. 'Time to unmask, my love.' Her mask dropped off, but he of course did nothing. 'Come, come,' she said. 'You must take your mask off too.'

It was a command and of course as a robot he had to obey. With a flourish he pulled off his face.

Carol Ann screamed first, then burned with anger.

'What sort of scheme is this, you animated tin can? Answer.'

'It was love dear one. Love that brought me here tonight and sent me to your arms.' The answer was true enough, though Filer couched it in the terms of his disguise.

When the soft words of her darling came out of the harsh mouth of the electronic speaker Carol Ann screamed again. She knew she had been made a fool of.

'Who sent you here like this, answer. What is the meaning of this disguise, answer. ANSWER! ANSWER! you articulated pile of cams and rods!'

Filer tried to sort out the questions and answer them one at a time, but she gave him no time to speak.

'It's the filthiest trick of all time, sending you here disguised as a man. You a robot. A nothing. A two-legged IBM machine with a victrola attached. Making believe you're a man when you're nothing but a robot.'

Suddenly Filer was on his feet, the words crackling and mechanical from his speaker.

'I'm a robot.'

The gentle voice of love was gone and replaced by that of mechanical despair. Thought chased thought through the whirling electronic circuits of his brain and they were all the same thought.

I'm a robot – a robot – I must have forgotten I was a robot – what can a robot be doing here with a woman – a

*robot can't kiss a woman – a woman can't love a robot –
yet she said she loved me – yet I'm a robot – a robot....*

With a mechanical shudder he turned from the girl and
clanked away. With each step his steel fingers plucked at
his clothes and plastic flesh until they came away in shards
and pieces. Fragments of cloth marked his trail away from
the woman and within a hundred paces he was as steel-
naked as the day he was built. Through the garden and
down to the street he went, the thoughts in his head going
in ever tighter circles.

It was uncontrolled feedback and soon his body followed
his brain. His legs went faster, his motors whirled more
rapidly, and the central lubrication pump in his thorax
churned like a mad thing.

Then, with a single metallic screech, he raised both arms
and plunged forward. His head hit a corner of a stair and
the granite point thrust into the thin casing. Metal groun-
ded to metal and all the complex circuits that made up his
brain were instantly discharged.

Robot Filer 13B-445-K was quite dead.

That was what the report read that the mechanic sent in
the following day. Not dead, but permanently impaired, to
be disposed of. Yet, strangely enough, that wasn't what this
same man said when he examined the metallic corpse.

A second mechanic had helped in the examination. It
was he who had spun off the bolts and pulled out the
damaged lubrication pump.

'Here's the trouble,' he had announced. 'Malfunction in
the pump. Piston broke, jammed the pump, the knees
locked from lack of oil – then the robot fell and shorted out
his brains.'

The first mechanic wiped grease off his hands and examined the faulty pump. Then he looked from it to the
gaping hole in the chest.

'You could almost say he died of a broken heart.'

They both laughed and he threw the pump into the
corner with all the other cracked, dirty, broken and discarded machinery.

Overswing is a human tendency. When a new driver sees the car veering from a straight line he twists the wheel back to correct the turn – but twists too far. The car turns in the opposite direction and the process is repeated. The automobile wiggles down the road like a snake, constantly correcting but never correct.

Overswing is also characteristic of human institutions. Periods of moral licentiousness are followed by those of puritan harshness.

Overswing is a trait of machines too, and is hidden behind such terms as undamped oscillation and negative feedback.

Robots are humanoid machines and there is a very good chance that they will be struck by this same malfunction. Individually, it is easily correctable. A single robot with difficulties will be noticed and repaired. But what can be done if the malfunction is inherent in the mechanism – and all the machines have the same malfunction? Can it even be noticed, much less corrected?

Robots are already well-entrenched in the operations of society and the administering of our laws. Robot clerks tick off the fines paid and send out summonses to defaulters. Robot accountants check income tax returns and respond with a rapidly flashing light to small errors and exaggerations. Robot eyes and sensitive detectors guard the security of our prisons. Robot voting machines accept our secret ballot and tally the results.

Is it not within the realm of possibility that robots will be handed more and more functions of government and administration, until there are no more to be given them – because they will have them all ... ?

I SEE YOU

The judge was impressive in his black robes, and omniscient in the chromium perfection of his skull. His voice rolled like the crack of doom; rich and penetrating.

'Carl Tritt, this court finds you guilty as charged. On 218, 2423 you did willfully and maliciously steal the payroll of the Marcrix Corporation, a sum totaling 318,000 cr., and did attempt to keep these same credits as your own. The sentence is twenty years.'

The black gavel fell with the precision of a pile driver and the sound bounced back and forth inside Carl's head. Twenty years. He clamped bloodless fingers on the steel bar of justice and looked up into the judge's electronic eyes. There was perhaps a glint of compassion, but no mercy there. The sentence had been passed and recorded in the Central Memory. There was no appeal.

A panel snapped open in the front of the judge's bench and exhibit 'A' slid out on a soundless piston. 318,000 cr., still in their original pay envelopes. The judge pointed as Carl slowly picked it up.

'Here is the money you stole – see that it is returned to the proper people.'

Carl shuffled out of the courtroom, the package clutched weakly to his chest, sunk in a sodden despair. The street outside was washed with a golden sunlight that he could not see, for his depression shadowed it with the deepest gloom.

His throat was sore and his eyes burned. If he had not been an adult male citizen, age 25, he might have cried. But 25-year-old adult males do not cry. Instead he swallowed heavily a few times.

A twenty-year sentence – it couldn't be believed. *Why me?* Of all the people in the world why did *he* have to receive a sentence severe as that? His well-trained conscience instantly shot back the answer. *Because you stole money.* He shied away from that unpleasant thought and stumbled on.

Unshed tears swam in his eyes and trickled back into his nose and down his throat. Forgetting in his misery where he was, he choked a bit. Then spat heavily.

Even as the saliva hit the spotless sidewalk, a waste can twenty feet away stirred into life. It rotated on hidden wheels and soundlessly rolled towards him. In shocked horror Carl pressed the back of his hand to his mouth. Too late to stop what was already done.

A flexible arm licked out and quickly swabbed the sidewalk clean. Then the can squatted like a mechanical Buddha while a speaker rasped to life in its metal insides. A tinny metallic voice addressed Carl.

'Carl Tritt, you have violated Local Ordinance #bd-14-668 by expectorating on a public sidewalk. The sentence is two days. Your total sentence is now twenty years and two days.'

Two other pedestrians had stopped behind Carl, listening with gaping mouths as sentence was passed. Carl could almost hear their thought. *A sentenced man. Think of that! Over twenty years sentence!* They bugged their eyes at him in a mixture of fascination and distaste.

Carl rushed away, the package clutched to his chest and his face flushed red with shame. The sentenced men on video had always seemed so funny. How they fell down and acted bewildered when a door wouldn't open for them.

It didn't seem so funny now.

The rest of that day crept by in a fog of dejection. He had a vague recollection of his visit to the Marcrix Corporation to return his stolen money. They had been kind and understanding, and he had fled in embarrassment. All the kindness in the world wouldn't reprieve his sentence.

He wandered vaguely in the streets after that, until he

was exhausted. Then he had seen the bar. Bright lights with
a fog of smoke inside, looking cheery and warm. Carl had
pushed at the door, and pushed again, while the people
inside had stopped talking and turned to watch him
through the glass. Then he had remembered the sentence
and realized the door wouldn't open. The people inside had
started laughing and he had run away. Lucky to get off
without a further sentence.

When he reached his apartment at last he was sobbing
with fatigue and unhappiness. The door opened to his
thumb and slammed behind him. This was a refuge at last.

Until he saw his packaged bags waiting for him.

Carl's video set hummed into life. He had never realized
before it could be controlled from a Central. The screen
stayed dark but the familiar voder voice of Sentence Control poured out.

'A selection of clothing and articles suitable for a sentenced man has been chosen for you. Your new address is
on your bags. Go there at once.'

It was too much. Carl knew without looking that his
camera and his books and model rockets – the hundred
other little things that meant something to him – were not
included in those bags. He ran into the kitchen, forcing
open the resisting door. The voice spoke from a speaker
concealed above the stove.

'What you are doing is in violation of the law. If you stop
at once your sentence will not be increased.'

The words meant nothing to him, he didn't want to hear
them. With frantic fingers he pulled the cupboard open and
reached for the bottle of whiskey in the back. The bottle
vanished through a trap door he had never noticed before,
brushing tantalizingly against his fingers as it dropped.

He stumbled down the hall and the voice droned on behind him. Five more days sentence for attempting to obtain
alcoholic beverages. Carl couldn't have cared less.

The cabs and buses wouldn't stop for him and the sub-
slide turnstile spat his coin back like something distasteful.
In the end he tottered the long blocks to his new quarters,

located in a part of town he had never known existed.

There was a calculated seediness about the block where he was to stay. Deliberately cracked sidewalks and dim lights. The dusty spiderwebs that hung in every niche had a definitely artificial look about them. He had to climb two flights of stairs, each step of which creaked with a different note, to reach his room. Without turning the light on he dropped his bags and stumbled forward. His shins cracked against a metal bed and he dropped gratefully into it. A blissful exhaustion put him to sleep.

When he awoke in the morning he didn't want to open his eyes. It had been a nightmare, he tried to tell himself, and he was safely out of it now. But the chill air in the room and the gray light filtering through his lids told him differently. With a sigh he abandoned the fantasy and looked around at his new home.

It was clean – and that was all that could be said for it. The bed, a chair, a built-in chest of drawers – these were the furnishings. A single unshielded bulb hung from the ceiling. On the wall opposite him was a large metal calendar sign. It read: *20 years, 5 days, 17 hours, 25 minutes.* While he watched the sign gave an audible click and the last number changed to 24.

Carl was too exhausted by the emotions of the previous day to care. The magnitude of his change still overwhelmed him. He settled back onto the bed in a half daze, only to be jolted up by a booming voice from the wall.

'Breakfast is now being served in the public dining room on the floor above. You have ten minutes.' The now familiar voice came this time from a giant speaker at least 5 feet across, and had lost all of its tinny quality. Carl obeyed without thinking.

The meal was drab but filling. There were other men and women in the dining room, all very interested in their food. He realized with a start that they were sentenced too. After that he kept his own eyes on his plate and returned quickly to his room.

As he entered the door the video pickup was pointing at

him from above the speaker. It followed him like a gun as he walked across the room. Like the speaker, it was the biggest pickup he had ever seen; a swiveled chrome tube with a glass eye on its end as big as his fist. A sentenced man is alone, yet never has privacy.

Without preliminary warning the speaker blasted and he gave a nervous start.

'Your new employment begins at 1800 hours today, here is the address.' A card leaped out of a slot below the calendar sign and dropped to the floor. Carl had to bend over and scratch at its edges to pick it up. The address meant nothing to him.

He had hours of time before he had to be there, and nothing else to do. The bed was nearby and inviting, he dropped wearily onto it.

Why had he stolen that damned payroll? He knew the answer. Because he had wanted things he could never afford on a telephone technician's salary. It had looked so tempting and fool proof. He damned the accident that had led him to it. The memory still tortured him.

It had been a routine addition of lines in one of the large office buildings.

When he first went there he had been by himself, he would not need the robots until after the preliminary survey was done. The phone circuits were in a service corridor just off the main lobby. His pass key let him in through the inconspicuous door and he switched on the light. A maze of wiring and junction boxes covered one wall, leading to cables that vanished down the corridor out of sight. Carl opened his wiring diagrams and began to trace leads. The rear wall seemed to be an ideal spot to attach the new boxes and he tapped it to see if it could take the heavy bolts. It was hollow.

Carl's first reaction was disgust. The job would be twice as difficult if the leads had to be extended. Then he felt a touch of curiosity as to what the wall was there for. It was just a panel he noticed on closer inspection, made up of snap-on sections fitted into place. With his screwdriver he pried one section out and saw what looked like a steel grid supporting metal plates. He had no idea of what their function was, and didn't really care now that his mild curiosity had been settled. After slipping the panel back into place he went on with his work. A few hours later he looked at his watch, then dropped his tools for lunch.

The first thing he saw when he stepped back into the lobby was the bank cart.

Walking as close as he was, Carl couldn't help but notice the two guards who were taking thick envelopes from the cart and putting them into a bank of lockers set into the wall. One envelope to each locker, then a slam of the thick door to seal it shut. Besides a momentary pang at the sight of all that money Carl had no reaction.

Only when he came back from lunch did he stop suddenly as a thought struck him. He hesitated a fraction of a moment, then went on. No one had noticed him. As he entered the corridor again he looked surreptitiously at the messenger who was opening one of the lockers. When Carl had closed the door behind him and checked the relative position of the wall with his eyes he knew he was right.

What he had thought was a metal grid with plates was really the backs of the lockers and their framework of supports. The carefully sealed lockers in the lobby had unguarded backs that faced into the service corridor.

He realized at once that he should do nothing at the time, nor act in any way to arouse suspicion. He did, however, make sure that the service robots came in through the other end of the corridor that opened onto a deserted hallway at the rear of the building where he had made a careful examination of the hall. Carl even managed to make himself forget about the lockers for over six months.

After that he began to make his plans. Casual observation at odd times gave him all the facts he needed. The lockers contained payrolls for a number of large companies in the building. The bank guards deposited the money at noon every Friday. No envelopes were ever picked up before one P.M. at the earliest. Carl noticed what seemed to be the thickest envelope and made his plans accordingly.

Everything went like clockwork. At ten minutes to twelve on a Friday he finished a job he was working on and left. He carried his toolbox with him. Exactly ten minutes later he entered the rear door of the corridor without being seen. His hands were covered with transparent and nearly invisible gloves. By 12:10 he had the panel off and the blade of a long screwdriver pressed against the back of the selected locker; the handle of the screwdriver held to the bone behind his ear. There was no sound of closing doors so he knew the bank men had finished and gone.

The needle flame of his torch ate through the steel panel like soft cheese. He excised a neat circle of metal and pulled it free. Beating out a smoldering spot on the money envelope, he transferred it to another envelope from his toolbox. This envelope he had addressed to himself and was already stamped. One minute after leaving the building he would have the envelope in the mail and would be a rich man.

Carefully checking, he put all the tools and the envelope back into his toolbox and strode away. At exactly 12:35 he left through the rear corridor door and locked it behind him. The corridor was still empty, so he took the extra seconds to jimmy the door open with a tool from his pocket. Plenty of people had keys to that door, but it didn't hurt to widen the odds a bit.

Carl was actually whistling when he walked out into the street.

Then the peace officer took him by the arm.

'You are under arrest for theft,' the officer told him in a calm voice.

The shock stopped him in his tracks and he almost wished it had stopped his heart the same way. He had never planned to be caught and never considered the consequences. Fear and shame made him stumble as the policeman led him to the waiting car. The crowd watched in fascinated amazement.

When the evidence had been produced at his trial he found out, a little late, what his mistake had been. Because of the wiring and conduits in the corridor it was equipped with infra-red thermocouples. The heat of his torch had activated the alarm and an observer at Fire Central had looked through one of their video pickups in the tunnel. He had expected to see a short circuit and had been quite surprised to see Carl removing the money. His surprise had not prevented him from notifying the police. Carl had cursed fate under his breath.

The grating voice of the speaker cut through Carl's bad tasting memories.

'1730 hours. It is time for you to leave for your employment.'

Wearily, Carl pulled on his shoes, checked the address, and left for his new job. It took him almost the full half hour to walk there. He wasn't surprised in the slightest when the address turned out to be the Department of Sanitation.

'You'll catch on fast,' the elderly and worn supervisor told him. 'Just go through this list and kind of get acquainted with it. Your truck will be along in a moment.'

The list was in reality a thick volume of lists, of all kinds of waste materials. Apparently everything in the world that could be discarded was in the book. And each item was followed by a key number. These numbers ran from one to thirteen and seemed to be the entire purpose of the volume. While Carl was puzzling over their meaning there was a sudden roar of a heavy motor. A giant robot-operated truck pulled up the ramp and ground to a stop near them.

'Garbage truck,' the supervisor said wearily. 'She's all yours.'

Carl had always known there were garbage trucks, but of course he had never seen one. It was a bulky, shining cylinder over twenty metres long. A robot driver was built into the cab. Thirty other robots stood on foot-steps along the sides. The supervisor led the way to the rear of the truck and pointed to the gaping mouth of the receiving bin.

'Robots pick up the garbage and junk and load it in there,' he said. 'Then they press one of these here thirteen buttons keying whatever they have dumped into one of the thirteen bins inside the truck. They're just plain lifting robots and not too brainy, but good enough to recognize most things they pick up. But not all the time. That's where you come in, riding along right there.'

The grimy thumb was now aiming at a transparent-walled cubicle that also projected from the back of the truck. There was a padded seat inside, facing a shelf set with thirteen buttons.

'You sit there, just as cozy as a bug in a rug I might say, ready to do your duty at any given moment. Which is whenever one of the robots finds something it can't identify straight off. So it puts whatever it is into the hopper outside your window. You give it a good look, check the list for the proper category if you're not sure, then press the right button and in she goes. It may sound difficult at first, but you'll soon catch onto the ropes.'

'Oh, it sounds complicated all right,' Carl said, with a dull feeling in his gut as he climbed into his turret, 'but I'll try and get used to it.'

The weight of his body closed a hidden switch in the chair, and the truck growled forward. Carl scowled down unhappily at the roadway streaming out slowly from behind the wheels, as he rode into the darkness, sitting in his transparent boil on the back-side of the truck.

It was dull beyond imagining. The garbage truck followed a programmed route that led through the commercial and freightways of the city. There were few other trucks moving at that hour of the night, and they were all robot driven. Carl saw no other human being. He *was* snug as a bug. A human flea being whirled around inside the complex machine of the city. Every few minutes the truck would stop, the robots clatter off, then return with their loads. The containers dumped, the robots leaped back to their footplates, and the truck was off once more.

An hour passed before he had his first decision to make. A robot stopped in mid-dump, ground its gears a moment, then dropped a dead cat into Carl's hopper. Carl stared at it with horror. The cat stared back with wide, sightless eyes, its lips drawn back in a fierce grin. It was the first corpse Carl had ever seen. Something heavy had dropped on the cat, reducing the lower part of its body to paper-thinness. With an effort he wrenched his eyes away and jerked the book open.

Castings ... Cast Iron ... Cats (dead) ... Very, very much dead. There was the bin number. Nine. One bin per life. After the ninth life – the ninth bin. He didn't find the thought very funny. A fierce jab at button 9 and the cat whisked from sight with a last flourish of its paw. He repressed the sudden desire to wave back.

After the cat boredom set in with a vengeance. Hours dragged slowly by and still his hopper was empty. The truck rumbled forward and stopped. Forward and stop. The motion lulled him and he was tired. He leaned forward and laid his head gently on the list of varieties of garbage, his eyes closed.

'Sleeping is forbidden while at work. This is warning number one.'

The hatefully familiar voice blasted from behind his head and he started with surprise. He hadn't noticed the pickup and speaker next to the door. Even here, riding a garbage truck to eternity, the machine watched him. Bitter anger kept him awake for the duration of the round.

Days came and went after that in a gray monotony, the large calendar on the wall of his room ticking them off one by one. But not fast enough. It now read 19 years, 322 days, 8 hours, 16 minutes. Not fast enough. There was no more interest in his life. As a sentenced man there were very few things he could do in his free time. All forms of entertainment were closed to him. He could gain admittance – through a side door – to only a certain section of the library. After one futile trip there, pawing through the inspirational texts and moral histories, he never returned.

*

Each night he went to work. After returning he slept as long as he could. After that he just lay on his bed, smoking his tiny allotment of cigarettes, and listening to the seconds being ticked off his sentence.

Carl tried to convince himself that he could stand twenty years in this kind of existence. But a growing knot of tension in his stomach told him differently.

This was before the accident. The accident changed everything.

A night like any other night. The garbage truck stopped at an industrial site and the robots scurried out for their loads. Nearby was a cross-country tanker, taking on some liquid through a flexible hose. Carl gave it bored notice only because there was a human driver in the cab of the truck. That meant the cargo was dangerous in some way, robot drivers being forbidden by law from handling certain loads. He idly noticed the driver open the door and start to step out. When the man was halfway out he remembered something, turned back and reached for it.

For a short moment the driver brushed against the starter button. The truck was in gear and lurched forward a few feet. The man quickly pulled away – but it was too late.

The movement had been enough to put a strain on the hose. It stretched – the supporting arm bent – then it broke free from the truck at the coupling. The hose whipped back and forth, spraying greenish liquid over the truck and the cab, before an automatic cut-out turned off the flow.

This had taken only an instant. The driver turned back and stared with horror-widened eyes at the fluid dripping over the truck's hood. It was steaming slightly.

With a swooshing roar it burst into fire, and the entire front of the truck was covered with flame. The driver invisible behind the burning curtain.

Before being sentenced Carl had always worked with robot assistance. He knew what to say and how to say it to get instant obedience. Bursting from his cubicle he slapped one of the garbage robots on its metal shoulder and shouted an order. The robot dropped a can it was emptying and ran at full speed for the truck, diving into the flames.

More important than the driver, was the open port on top of the truck. If the flames should reach it the entire truck would go up – showering the street with burning liquid.

Swathed in flame, the robot climbed the ladder on the truck's side. One burning hand reached up and flipped the self-sealing lid shut. The robot started back down through the flames, but stopped suddenly as the fierce heat burned at its controls. For a few seconds it vibrated rapidly like a man in pain, then collapsed. Destroyed.

Carl was running towards the truck himself, guiding two more of his robots. The flames still wrapped the cab, seeping in through the partly open door. Thin screams of pain came from inside. Under Carl's directions one robot pulled the door open and the other dived in. Bent double, protecting the man's body with its own, the robot pulled the driver out. The flames had charred his legs to shapeless masses and his clothes were on fire. Carl beat out the flames with his hands as the robot dragged the driver clear.

The instant the fire had started, automatic alarms had gone off. Fire and rescue teams plunged toward the scene. Carl had just put out the last of the flames on the unconscious man's body when they arrived. A wash of foam instantly killed the fire. An ambulance jerked to a stop and two robot stretcher-bearers popped out of it. A human doctor followed. He took one look at the burned driver and whistled.

'Really cooked!'

He grabbed a pressurized container from the stretcher-bearer and sprayed jelly-like burn dressing over the driver's legs. Before he had finished the other robot snapped open a medical kit and proffered it. The doctor made quick adjustments on a multiple syringe, then gave the injection. It was all very fast and efficient.

As soon as the stretcher-bearers had carried the burned driver into the ambulance, it jumped forward. The doctor mumbled instruction to the hospital into his lapel radio. Only then did he turn his attention to Carl.

'Let's see those hands,' he said.

Everything had happened with such speed that Carl had scarcely noticed his burns. Only now did he glance down at the scorched skin and feel sharp pain. The blood drained from his face and he swayed.

'Easy does it,' the doctor said, helping him sit down on the ground. 'They're not as bad as they look. Have new skin on them in a couple of days.' His hands were busy while he talked and there was the sudden prick of a needle in Carl's arm. The pain ebbed away.

The shot made things hazy after that. Carl had vague memories of riding to the hospital in a police car. Then the grateful comfort of a cool bed. They must have given him another shot then because the next thing he knew it was morning.

That week in the hospital was like a vacation for Carl. Either the staff didn't know of his sentenced status or it didn't make any difference. He received the same treatment as the other patients. While the accelerated grafts covered his hands and forearms with new skin, he relaxed in the luxury of the soft bed and varied food. The same drugs that kept the pain away prevented his worry about returning to the outside world. He was also pleased to hear that the burned driver would recover.

On the morning of the eighth day the staff dermatologist prodded the new skin and smiled. 'Good job of recovery, Tritt,' he said.

'Looks like you'll be leaving us today. I'll have them fill out the forms and send for your clothes.'

The old knot of tension returned to Carl's stomach as he thought of what waited for him outside. It seemed doubly hard now that he had been away for a few days. Yet there was nothing else he could possibly do. He dressed as slowly as he could, stretching the free time remaining as much as possible.

As he started down the corridor a nurse waved him over.

'Mr. Skarvy would like to see you – in here.'

Skarvy. That was the name of the truck driver. Carl followed her into the room where the burly driver sat up in bed. His big body looked strange somehow, until Carl realized there was no long bulge under the blankets. The man had no legs.

'Chopped 'em both off at the hips,' Skarvy said when he noticed Carl's gaze. He smiled. 'Don't let it bother you. Don't bother me none. They planted the regen-buds and they tell me in less than a year I'll have legs again, good as new. Suits me fine. Better than staying in that truck and frying.' He hitched himself up in the bed, an intense expression on his face.

'They showed me the films Fire Central made through one of their pick-ups on the spot. Saw the whole thing. Almost upchucked when I saw what I looked like when you dragged me out.' He pushed out a meaty hand and pumped Carl's. 'I want to thank you for doing what you done. Taking a chance like that.' Carl could only smile foolishly.

'I want to shake your hand,' Skarvy said. 'Even if you are a sentenced man.'

Carl pulled his hand free and left. Not trusting himself to say anything. The last week *had* been a dream. And a foolish one. He was still sentenced and would be for years to come. An outcast of society who never left it.

When he pushed open the door to his drab room the all too-familiar voice boomed out of the speaker.

'Carl Tritt. You have missed seven days of your work assignment, in addition there is an incomplete day, only partially worked. This time would normally not be deducted from your sentence. There is however precedent in allowing deduction of this time and it will be allowed against your total sentence.' The decision made, the numbers clicked over busily on his calendar.

'Thanks for nothing,' Carl said and dropped wearily on his bed. The monotonous voder voice went on, ignoring his interruption.

'In addition, an award has been made. Under Sentence

Diminution Regulations your act of personal heroism, risking your own life to save another's, is recognized as a prosocial act and so treated. The award is three years off your sentence.'

Carl was on his feet, staring unbelievingly at the speaker. Was it some trick? Yet as he watched the calendar mechanism ground gears briefly and the year numbers slowly turned over. 18 ... 17 ... 16 ... The whirring stopped.

Just like that. Three years off his sentence. It didn't seem possible – yet there were the numbers to prove that it was.

'Sentence Control!' he shouted. 'Listen to me! What happened? I mean how can a sentence be reduced by this award business? I never heard anything about it before?'

'Sentence reduction is never mentioned in public life,' the speaker said flatly. 'This might encourage people to break the law, since threat of sentence is considered a deterrent. Normally a sentenced person is not told of sentence reduction until after their first year. Your case however is exceptional since you were awarded reduction before the end of said year.'

'How can I find out more about sentence reduction?' Carl asked eagerly.

The speaker hummed for a moment, then the voice crackled out again. 'Your Sentence Advisor is Mr. Prisbi. He will advise you in whatever is to be done. You have an appointment for 1300 hours tomorrow. Here is his address.'

The machine clicked and spat out a card. Carl was waiting for it this time and caught it before it hit the floor. He held it carefully, almost lovingly. Three years off his sentence and tomorrow he would find out what else he could do to reduce it even more.

Of course he was early, almost a full hour before he was due. The robot-receptionist kept him seated in the outer office until the exact minute of his appointment. When he heard the door lock finally click open he almost jumped to it. Forcing himself to go slow, he entered the office.

Prisbi, the Sentence Advisor, looked like a preserved fish peering through the bottom of a bottle. He was dumpy fat, with dead white skin and lumpy features that had been squeezed up like putty from the fat underneath. His eyes were magnified pupils that peered unblinkingly through eye-glass lenses almost as thick as they were wide. In a world where contact lenses were the norm, his vision was so bad it could not be corrected by the tiny lenses. Instead he wore the heavy-framed, anachronistic spectacles, perched insecurely on his puffy nose.

Prisbi did not smile or say a word when Carl entered the door. He kept his eyes fixed steadily on him as he walked the length of the room. They reminded Carl of the video scanners he had grown to hate, and he shook the idea away.

'My name is . . .' he began.

'I know your name, Tritt,' Prisbi rasped. The voice seemed too coarse to have come from those soft lips. 'Now sit down in that chair – there.' He jerked his pen at a hard metal chair that faced his desk.

Carl sat down and immediately blinked away from the strong lights that focused on his face. He tried to slide the chair back, until he realized it was fastened to the floor. He just sat then and waited for Prisbi to begin.

Prisbi finally lowered his glassy gaze and picked up a file of papers from his desk. He riffled through them for a full minute before speaking.

'Very strange record, Tritt,' he finally grated out. 'Can't say that I like it at all. Don't even know why Control gave you permission to be here. But since you are – tell me why.'

It was an effort to smile but Carl did. 'Well you see, I was awarded a three-year reduction in sentence. This is the first I ever heard of sentence reduction. Control sent me here, said you would give me more information.'

'A complete waste of time,' Prisbi said, throwing the papers down onto the desk. 'You aren't eligible for sentence reduction until after you've finished your first year of sentence. You have almost ten months to go. Come back then and I'll explain. You can leave.'

Carl didn't move. His hands were clenched tight in his lap as he fought for control. He squinted against the light, looking at Prisbi's unresponsive face.

'But you see I have already *had* sentence reduction. Perhaps that's why Control told me to come—'

'Don't try and teach me the law,' Prisbi growled coldly. 'I'm here to teach it to you. All right I'll explain. Though it's of absolutely no value now. When you finish your first year of sentence – a *real* year of *work* at your assigned job – you are eligible for reduction. You may apply then for other work that carries a time premium. Dangerous jobs such as satellite repair, that take two days off your sentence for every day served. There are even certain positions in atomics that allow three days per day worked, though these are rare. In this way the sentenced man helps himself, learns social consciousness, and benefits society at the same time. Of course this doesn't apply to you yet.'

'Why not?' Carl was standing now, hammering on the table with his still tender hands. 'Why do I have to finish a year at that supid, made-work job? It's completely artificial, designed to torture, not to accomplish anything. The amount of work I do every night could be done in three seconds by a robot when the truck returned. Do you call that teaching social consciousness? Humiliating, boring work that—'

'Sit down, Tritt,' Prisbi shouted in a high, cracked voice. 'Don't you realize where you are? Or who I am? I tell you what to do. You don't say anything to me outside of *yes, sir* or *no, sir*. I say you must finish your primary year of work, then return here. That is an order.'

'I say you're wrong,' Carl shouted. 'I'll go over your head – see your superiors – you just can't decide my life away like that!'

Prisbi was standing now too, a twisted grimace splitting his face in a caricature of a smile. He roared at Carl.

'You can't go over my head or appeal to anyone else – I have the last word! You hear that? *I tell you what to do.* I say you work – and you're going to work. You doubt that?

You doubt what I can do?' There was a bubble of froth on his pale lips now. 'I say you have shouted at me and used insulting language and threatened me, and the record will bear me out!'

Prisbi fumbled on his desk until he found a microphone. He raised it, trembling, to his mouth and pressed the button.

'This is Sentence Advisor Prisbi. For actions unbecoming a sentenced man when addressing a Sentence Advisor, I recommend Carl Tritt's sentence be increased by one week.'

The answer was instantaneous. The Sentence Control speaker on the wall spoke in its usual voder tones. 'Sentence approved. Carl Tritt, seven days have been added to your sentence, bringing it to a total of sixteen years ...'

The words droned on, but Carl wasn't listening. He was staring down a red tunnel of hatred. The only thing he was aware of in the entire world was the pasty white face of Advisor Prisbi.

'You ... didn't have to do that,' he finally choked out. 'You don't have to make it worse for me when you're supposed to be helping me.' Sudden realization came to Carl. 'But you don't want to help me, do you? You enjoy playing God with sentenced men, twisting their lives in your hands—'

His voice was drowned out by Prisbi's, shouting into the microphone again ... *deliberate insults ... recommend a month be added to Carl Tritt's sentence....* Carl heard what the other man was saying. But he didn't care any more. He had tried hard to do it their way. He couldn't do it any longer. He hated the system, the men who designed it, the machines that enforced it. And most of all he hated the man before him, who was a summation of the whole rotten mess. At the end, for all his efforts, he had ended up in the hands of this pulpy sadist. It wasn't going to be that way at all.

'Take your glasses off,' he said in a low voice.

'What's that ... what?' Prisbi said. He had finished

shouting into the microphone and was breathing heavily.

'Don't bother,' Carl said reaching slowly across the table. 'I'll do it for you.' He pulled the man's glasses off and laid them gently on the table. Only then did Prisbi realize what was happening. *No* was all he could say, in a sudden outrush of breath.

Carl's fist landed square on those hated lips, broke them, broke the teeth behind them and knocked the man back over his chair onto the floor. The tender new skin on Carl's hand was torn and blood dripped down his fingers. He wasn't aware of it. He stood over the huddled, whimpering shape on the floor and laughed. Then he stumbled out of the office, shaken with laugher.

The robot-receptionist turned a coldly disapproving, glass and steel, face on him and said something. Still laughing he wrenched a heavy light stand from the floor and battered the shining face in. Clutching the lamp he went out into the hall.

Part of him screamed in terror at the enormity of what he had done, but just part of his mind. And this small voice was washed away by the hot wave of pleasure that surged through him. He was breaking the rules – *all* of the rules – this time. Breaking out of the cage that had trapped him all of his life.

As he rode down in the automatic elevator the laughter finally died away, and he wiped the dripping sweat from his face. A small voice scratched in his ear.

'Carl Tritt, you have committed violation of sentence and your sentence is hereby increased by . . .'

'Where are you!' he bellowed. 'Don't hide there and whine in my ear. Come out!' He peered closely at the wall of the car until he found the glass lens.

'You see me, do you?' he shouted at the lens. 'Well I see you too!' The lamp stand came down and crashed into the glass. Another blow tore through the thin metal and found the speaker. It expired with a squawk.

People ran from him in the street, but he didn't notice them. They were just victims the way he had been. It was the enemy he wanted to crush. Every video eye he saw caught a blow from the battered stand. He poked and tore until he silenced every speaker he passed. A score of battered and silent robots marked his passage.

It was inevitable that he should be caught. He neither thought about that nor cared very much. *This* was the moment he had been living for all his life. There was no battle song he could sing, he didn't know any. But there was one mildly smutty song he remembered from his school days. It would have to do. Roaring it at the top of his voice, Carl left a trail of destruction through the shining order of the city.

The speakers never stopped talking to Carl, and he silenced them as fast as he found them. His sentence mounted higher and higher with each act.

'... making a total of two hundred and twelve years, nineteen days and ...' The voice was suddenly cut off as some control circuit finally realized the impossibility of its statements. Carl was riding a moving ramp towards a freight level. He crouched, waiting for the voice to start again so he could seek it out and destroy it. A speaker rustled and he looked around for it.

'Carl Tritt, your sentence has exceeded the expected bounds of your life and is therefore meaningless ...'

'Always was meaningless,' he shouted back. 'I know that now. Now where are you? I'm going to get you!' The machine droned on steadily.

'... in such a case you are remanded for trial. Peace officers are now on their way to bring you in. You are ordered to go peacefully or ... GLILRK ...' The lamp stand smashed into the speaker.

'Send them,' Carl spat into the mass of tangled metal and wire. 'I'll take care of them too.'

The end was preordained. Followed by the ubiquitous eyes of Central, Carl could not run forever. The squad of officers cornered him on a lower level and closed in. Two of them were clubbed unconscious before they managed to get a knockout needle into his flesh.

The same courtroom and the same judge. Only this time there were two muscular human guards present to watch Carl. He didn't seem to need watching, slumped forward as he was against the bar of justice. White bandages covered the cuts and bruises.

A sudden humming came from the robot judge as he stirred to life. 'Order in the court,' he said, rapping the gavel once and returning it to its stand. 'Carl Tritt, this court finds you guilty...'

'What, again? Aren't you tired of that sort of thing yet?' Carl asked.

'Silence while sentence is being passed,' the judge said loudly and banged down again with the gavel. 'You are guilty of crimes too numerous to be expiated by sentencing. Therefore you are condemned to Personality Death. Psycho-surgery shall remove all traces of this personality from your body, until this personality is dead, dead, dead.'

'Not that,' Carl whimpered, leaning forward and stretching his arms out pleadingly towards the judge. 'Anything but that.'

Before either guard could act, Carl's whimper turned to a loud laugh as he swept the judge's gavel off the bench. Turning with it, he attacked the astonished guards. One dropped instantly as the gavel caught him behind the ear. The other struggled to get his gun out – then fell across the first man's limp body.

'Now judge,' Carl shouted with happiness, '*I* have the gavel, let's see what *I* do!' He swept around the end of the bench and hammered the judge's sleek metal head into a twisted ruin. The judge, merely an extension of the machinery of Central Control, made no attempt to defend itself.

There was the sound of running feet in the hall and someone pulled at the door. Carl had no plan. All he wanted to do was remain free and do as much damage as long as the fire of rebellion burned inside of him. There was only the single door into the courtroom. Carl glanced quickly around and his technician's eye noticed the access plate set in the wall behind the judge. He twisted the latch and kicked it open.

A video tube was watching him from a high corner of the courtroom, but that couldn't be helped. The machine could follow him wherever he went anyway. All he could do was try and stay ahead of the pursuit. He pulled himself through the access door as two robots burst into the courtroom.

'Carl Tritt, surrender at once. A further change has been ... has been ... Carl ... carl ... ca ...'

Listening to their voices through the thin metal door, Carl wondered what had happened. He hazarded a look. Both robots had ground to a halt and were making aimless motions. Their speakers rustled, but said nothing. After a few moments the random movements stopped. They turned at the same time, picked up the unconscious peace officers, and went out. The door closed behind them. Carl found it very puzzling. He watched for some minutes longer, until the door opened again. This time it was a tool-hung repair robot that trundled in. It moved over to the ruined judge and began dismantling it.

Closing the door quietly, Carl leaned against its cool metal and tried to understand what had happened. With the threat of immediate pursuit removed, he had time to think.

Why hadn't he been followed? Why had Central Control acted as if it didn't know his whereabouts? This omnipotent machine had scanning tubes in every square inch of the city, he had found that out. And it was hooked into the machines of the other cities of the world. There was no place it couldn't see. Or rather one place.

The thought hit him so suddenly he gasped. Then he looked around him. A tunnel of relays and controls stretched away from him, dimly lit by glow plates. It could be – yes it could be. *It had to be.*

There could be only one place in the entire world that Central Control could not look – inside its own central mechanism. Its memory and operating circuits. No machine with independent decision could repair its own thinking circuits. This would allow destructive negative feedback to be built up. An impaired circuit could only impair itself more, it couldn't possibly repair itself.

He was inside the brain circuits of Central Control. So as far as that city-embracing machine knew he had ceased to be. He existed nowhere the machine could see. The machine could see everywhere. Therefore he didn't exist. By this time all memory of him had been probably erased.

Slowly at first, then faster and faster, he walked down the corridor.

'Free!' he shouted. 'Really free – for the first time in my life. Free to do as I want, to watch the whole world and laugh at them!' A power and happiness flowed through him. He opened door after door, exulting in his new kingdom.

He was talking aloud, bubbling with happiness. 'I can have the repair robots that work on the circuits bring me food. Furniture, clothes – whatever I want. I can live here just as I please – do what I please.' The thought was wildly exciting. He threw open another door and stopped, rigid.

The room before him was tastefully furnished, just as he would have done it. Books, paintings on the walls, soft music coming from a hidden record player. Carl gaped at it. Until the voice spoke behind him.

'Of course it would be wonderful to live here,' the voice said. 'To be master of the city, have anything you want at your fingertips. But what makes you think, poor little man, that you are the *first* one to realize that? And to come here. And there is really only room for one you know.'

Carl turned slowly, very slowly, measuring the distance between himself and the other man who stood behind him in the doorway, weighing the chances of lashing out with the gavel he still clutched – before the other man could fire the gun he held in his hand.

In the interplanetary age robots will be as much an essential and commonplace of life as the kitchen sink is to the atomic age. But while being waited upon by his mechanical servants, man will find that he has to do a little serving in return. Mechanics are needed to attend to the most automatic airplanes. Automatic lighthouses must be installed and serviced. This need will not die out. Spaceships will have to find their way through their dark spatial ocean, just as surely as any other ship that ever sailed a terrestrial sea. Navigation will be ultra-refined and automated – but it will still be navigation. And it will need the assistance of fixed reference points. Beacons will be needed.

And beacons, no matter how solidly constructed, will occasionally fall into disrepair. . . .

THE REPAIRMAN

The Old Man had that look of intense glee on his face that meant someone was in for a very rough time. Since we were alone, it took no great feat of intelligence to figure it would be me. I talked first, bold attack being the best defense and so forth.

'I quit. Don't bother telling me what dirty job you have cooked up, because I have already quit and you do not want to reveal company secrets to me.'

The grin was even wider now and he actually chortled as he thumbed a button on his console. A thick legal document slid out of the delivery slot onto his desk.

'This is your contract,' he said. 'It tells how and when you will work. A steel-and-vanadium-bound contract that you couldn't crack with a molecular disruptor.'

I leaned out quickly, grabbed it and threw it into the air with a single motion. Before it could fall, I had my Solar out and, with a wide-angle shot, burned the contract to ashes.

The Old Man pressed the button again and another contract slid out on his desk. If possible, the smile was still wider now.

'I should have said a *duplicate* of your contract – like this one here.' He made a quick note on his secretary plate. 'I have deducted 13 credits from your salary for the cost of the duplicate – as well as a 100-credit fine for firing a Solar inside a building.'

I slumped, defeated, waiting for the blow to land. The Old Man fondled my contract.

'According to this document, you can't quit. Ever. Therefore I have a little job I know you'll enjoy. Repair job. The

Centauri beacon has shut down. It's a Mark III beacon...'

'*What* kind of beacon?' I asked him. I have repaired hyperspace beacons from one arm of the Galaxy to the other and was sure I had worked on every type or model made. But I had never heard of this kind.

'Mark III,' the Old Man repeated with sly humor. 'I never heard of it either until Records dug up the specs. They found them buried in the back of their oldest warehouse. This was the earliest type of beacon ever built – by Earth, no less. Considering its location on one of the Proxima Centuri planets, it might very well be the first beacon.'

I looked at the blueprints he handed me and felt my eyes glaze with horror. 'It's a monstrosity! It looks more like a distillery than a beacon – must be at least a few hundred meters high. I'm a repairman, not an archeologist. This pile of junk is over 2000 years old. Just forget about it and build a new one.'

The Old Man leaned over his desk, breathing into my face. 'It would take a year to install a new beacon – besides being too expensive – and this relic is on one of the main routes. We have ships making fifteen-light-year detours now.'

He leaned back, wiped his hands on his handkerchief and gave me Lecture Forty-four on Company Duty and My Troubles.

'This department is officially called Maintenance and Repair, when it really should be called trouble-shooting. Hyperspace beacons are made to last forever – or damn close to it. When one of them breaks down, it is *never* an accident, and repairing the thing is *never* a matter of just plugging in a new part.'

He was telling *me* – the guy who did the job while he sat back on his fat paycheck in an air-conditioned office.

He rambled on. 'How I wish that were all it took! I would have a fleet of parts ships and junior mechanics to install them. But it's not like that at all. I have a fleet of expensive ships that are equipped to do almost anything – manned by a bunch of irresponsibles like *you*.'

I nodded moodily at his pointing finger.

'How I wish I could fire you all! Combination space-jockeys, mechanics, engineers, soldiers, con-men and anything else it takes to do the repairs. I have to browbeat, bribe, blackmail and bulldoze you thugs into doing a simple job. If you think you're fed up, just think how I feel. But the ships must go through! The beacons must operate!'

I recognized this deathless line as the curtain speech and crawled to my feet. He threw the Mark III file at me and went back to scratching in his papers. Just as I reached the door, he looked up and impaled me on his finger again.

'And don't get any fancy ideas about jumping your contract. We can attach that bank account of yours on Algol II long before you could draw the money out.'

I smiled, a little weakly, I'm afraid, as if I had never meant to keep that account a secret. His spies were getting more efficient every day. Walking down the hall, I tried to figure a way to transfer the money without his catching on – and knew at the same time he was figuring a way to outfigure me.

It was all very depressing, so I stopped for a drink, then went on to the spaceport.

By the time the ship was serviced, I had a course charted. The nearest beacon to the broken-down Proxima Centauri Beacon was on one of the planets of Beta Circinus and I headed there first, a short trip of only about nine days in hyperspace.

To understand the importance of the beacons, you have to understand hyperspace. Not that many people do, but it is easy enough to understand that in this *non*-space the regular rules don't apply. Speed and measurements are a matter of relationship, not constant facts like the fixed universe.

The first ships to enter hyperspace had no place to go – and no way to even tell if they had been moved. The beacons solved that problem and opened the entire universe. They are built on planets and generate tremendous amounts of power. This power is turned into radiation that is punched through into hyperspace. Every beacon has a code signal as part of its radiation and represents a measurable point in hyperspace. Triangulation and quadrature of the beacons works for navigation – only it follows its own rules. The rules are complex and variable, but they are still rules that a navigator can follow.

For a hyperspace jump, you need at least four beacons for an accurate fix. For long jumps, navigators use as many as seven or eight. So every beacon is important and every one has to keep operating. That is where I and the other trouble-shooters came in.

We travel in well-stocked ships that carry a little bit of everything; only one man to a ship because that is all it takes to operate the overly efficient repair machinery. Due to the very nature of our job, we spend most of our time just rocketing through normal space. After all, when a beacon breaks down, how do you find it?

Not through hyperspace. All you can do is approach as close as you can by using other beacons, then finish the trip in normal space. This can take months, and often does.

This job didn't turn out to be quite that bad. I zeroed on the Beta Circinus beacon and ran a complicated eight-point problem through the navigator, using every beacon I could get an accurate fix on. The computer gave me a course with an estimated point-of-arrival as well as a built-in safety factor I never could eliminate from the machine.

I would much rather take a chance of breaking through near some star than spend time just barreling through normal space, but apparently Tech knows this, too. They had a safety factor built into the computer so you couldn't end up inside a sun no matter how hard you tried. I'm sure there was no humaneness in this decision. They just didn't want to lose the ship.

It was a twenty-hour jump, ship's time, and I came through in the middle of nowhere. The robot analyzer chuckled to itself and scanned all the stars, comparing them to the spectra of Proxima Centauri. It finally rang a bell and blinked a light. I peeped through the eyepiece.

A last reading with the photocell gave me the apparent magnitude and a comparison with its absolute magnitude showed its distance. Not as bad as I had thought – a six-week run, give or take a few days. After feeding a course tape into the robot pilot, I strapped into the acceleration tank and went to sleep.

The time went fast. I rebuilt my camera for about the twentieth time and just about finished a correspondence course in nucleonics. Most repairmen take these courses. They have a value in themselves, because you never know what bit of odd information will come in handy. Not only that, the company grades your pay by the number of specialties you can handle. All this, with some oil painting and free-fall workouts in the gym, passed the time. I was asleep when the alarm went off that announced planetary distance.

Planet two, where the beacon was situated according to the old charts, was a mushy-looking, wet kind of globe. I worked hard to make sense out of the ancient directions and finally located the right area. Staying outside the atmosphere, I sent a Flying Eye down to look things over. In this business, you learn early when and where to risk your own skin. The Eye would be good enough for the preliminary survey.

The old boys had enough brains to choose a traceable site for the beacon, equidistant on a line between two of the most prominent mountain peaks. I located the peaks easily enough and started the Eye out from the first peak and kept it on a course directly toward the second. There was a nose and tail radar in the Eye and I fed their signals into a scope as an amplitude curve. When the two peaks coincided, I spun the Eye controls and dived the thing down.

I cut out the radar and cut in the nose orthicon and sat back to watch the beacon appear on the screen.

The image blinked, focused – and a great damn pyramid swam into view. I cursed and wheeled the Eye in circles, scanning the surrounding country. It was flat, marshy-bottom land without a bump. The only thing within a ten-mile circle was this pyramid – and that definitely wasn't my beacon.

Or was it?

I dived the Eye lower. The pyramid was a crude-looking thing of undressed stone, without carvings or decorations. There was a shimmer of light from the top and I took a closer look at it. On the peak of the pyramid was a hollow basin filled with water. When I saw that, something clicked in my mind.

Locking the Eye in a circular course, I dug through the Mark III plans – and there it was. The beacon had a pre-cipitating field and a basin on top of it for water; this was used to cool the reactor that powered the monstrosity. If the water was still there, the beacon was still there – inside the pyramid. The natives, who, of course, weren't even mentioned by the idiots who constructed the thing, had built a nice heavy, thick stone pyramid around the beacon.

I took another look at the screen and realized that I had locked the Eye into a circular orbit about twenty feet above the pyramid. The summit of the stone pile was now covered with lizards of some type, apparently the local life-form. They had what looked like throwing sticks and arbalasts and were trying to shoot down the Eye, a cloud of arrows and rocks flying in every direction.

I pulled the Eye straight up and away and threw in the control circuit that would return it automatically to the ship.

Then I went to the galley for a long, strong drink. My beacon was not only locked inside a mountain of hand-made stone, but I had managed to irritate the things who had built the pyramid. A great beginning for a job and one clearly designed to drive a stronger man than me to the bottle.

Normally, a repairman stays away from native cultures. They are poison. Anthropologists may not mind being dis-sected for their science, but a repairman wants to make no sacrifices of any kind for his job. For this reason, most beacons are built on uninhabited planets. If a beacon *has* to go on a planet with a culture, it is usually built in some inaccessible place.

Why this beacon had been built within reach of the local claws, I had yet to find out. But that would come in time. The first thing to do was to make contact. To make contact, you have to know the local language.

And, for *that*, I had long before worked out a system that was foolproof.

I had a pryeye of my own construction. It looked like a piece of rock about a foot long. Once on the ground, it would never be noticed, though it was a little disconcerting to see it float by. I located a lizard town about a thousand kilometers from the pyramid and dropped the Eye. It swished down and landed at night in the bank of the local mud wallow. This was a favorite spot that drew a good crowd during the day. In the morning, when the first wallowers arrived, I flipped on the recorder.

After about five of the local days, I had a sea of native conversation in the memory bank of the machine translator and had tagged a few expressions. This is fairly easy to do when you have a machine memory to work with. One of the lizards gargled at another one and the second one turned around. I tagged this expression with the phrase, 'Hey, George!' and waited my chance to use it. Later the same day, I caught one of them alone and shouted 'Hey, George!' at him. It gurgled out through the speaker in the local tongue and he turned around.

When you get enough reference phrases like this in the memory bank, the MT brain takes over and starts filling in the missing pieces. As soon as the MT could give a running translation of any conversation it heard, I figured it was time to make a contact.

I found him easily enough. He was the Centaurian version of a goat-boy – he herded a particularly loathsome form of local life in the swamps outside the town. I had one of the working Eyes dig a cave in an outcropping rock and wait for him.

When he passed next day, I whispered into the mike:
'Welcome, O Goat-boy Grandson! This is your grand-
father's spirit speaking from paradise.' This fitted in with
what I could make out of the local religion.

Goat-boy stopped as if he'd been shot. Before he could
move, I pushed a switch and a handful of the local cur-
rency, wampun-type shells, rolled out of the cave and
landed at his feet.

'Here is some money from paradise, because you have
been a good boy.' Not really from paradise – I had lifted it
from the treasury the night before. 'Come back tomorrow
and we will talk some more,' I called after the fleeing
figure. I was pleased to notice that he took the cash before
taking off.

After that, Grandpa in paradise had many heart-to-heart
talks with Grandson, who found the heavenly loot more
than he could resist. Grandpa had been out of touch with
things since his death and Goat-boy happily filled him in.

I learned all I needed to know of the history, past and
recent, and it wasn't nice.

In addition to the pyramid being around the beacon,
there was a nice little religious war going on around the
pyramid.

It all began with the land bridge. Apparently the local
lizards had been living in the distant swamps when the
beacon had been built, but the builders hadn't thought
much of them. They were a low type and confined to a
distant continent. The idea that the race would develop and
might reach *this* continent never occurred to the beacon
mechanics. Which is, of course, what happened.

A little geological turnover, a swampy land bridge
formed in the right spot, and the lizards began to wander
up beacon valley. And found religion. A shiny metal temple
out of which poured a constant stream of magic water – the
reactor-cooling water pumped down from the atmosphere
condenser on the roof. The radioactivity in the water didn't
hurt the natives. It caused mutations that bred true.

A city was built around the temple and, through the centuries, the pyramid was put up around the beacon. A special branch of the priesthood served the temple. All went well until one of the priests violated the temple and destroyed the holy waters. There had been revolt, strife, murder and destruction since then. But still the holy waters would not flow. Now armed mobs fought around the temple each day and a new band of priests guarded the sacred fount.

And I had to walk into the middle of that mess and repair the thing.

It would have been easy enough if we were allowed a little mayhem. I could have had a lizard fry, fixed the beacon and taken off. Only 'native life-forms' were quite well protected. There were spy cells on my ship, all of which I hadn't found, that would cheerfully rat on me when I got back.

Diplomacy was called for. I sighed and dragged out the plastiflesh equipment.

Working from 3D snaps of Grandson, I modeled a passable reptile head over my own features. It was a little short in the jaw, me not having one of their toothy mandibles, but that was all right. I didn't have to look *exactly* like them, just something close, to soothe the native mind. It's logical. If I were an ignorant aborigine of Earth and I ran into a Spican, who looks like a two-foot gob of dried shellac, I would immediately leave the scene. However, if the Spican was wearing a suit of plastiflesh that looked remotely humanoid, I would at least stay and talk to him. This was what I was aiming to do with the Centaurians.

When the head was done, I peeled it off and attached it to an attractive suit of green plastic, complete with tail. I was really glad they had tails. The lizards didn't wear clothes and I wanted to take along a lot of electronic equipment. I built the tail over a metal frame that anchored around my waist. Then I filled the frame with all the equipment I would need and began to wire the suit.

When it was done, I tried it on in front of a full-length mirror. It was horrible but effective. The tail dragged me down in the rear and gave me a duck-waddle, but that only helped the resemblance.

That night I took the ship down into the hills nearest the pyramid, an out-of-the-way dry spot where the amphibious natives would never go. A little before dawn, the Eye hooked onto my shoulders and we sailed straight up. We hovered above the temple at about 2000 meters, until it was light, then dropped down.

It must have been a grand sight. The Eye was camouflaged to look like a flying lizard, sort of a cardboard pterodactyl, and the slowly flapping wings obviously had nothing to do with our flight. But it was impressive enough for the natives. The first one that spotted me screamed and dropped over on his back. The others came running. They milled and mobbed and piled on top of one another, and by the time I had landed in the plaza fronting the temple the priesthood arrived.

I folded my arms in a regal stance. 'Greetings, O noble servers of the Great God,' I said. Of course I didn't say it out loud, just whispered softly enough for the throat mike to catch. This was radioed back to the MT and the translation shot back to a speaker in my jaws.

The natives chomped and rattled and the translation rolled out almost instantly. I had the volume turned up and the whole square echoed.

Some of the more credulous natives prostrated themselves and others fled screaming. One doubtful type raised a spear, but no one else tried that after the pterodactyl-eye picked him up and dropped him in the swamp. The priests were a hard-headed lot and weren't buying any lizards in a poke; they just stood and muttered. I had to take the offensive again.

'Begone, O faithful steed,' I said to the Eye, and pressed the control in my palm at the same time.

It took off straight up a bit faster than I wanted; little pieces of wind-torn plastic rained down. While the crowd was ogling this ascent, I walked through the temple doors.

'I would talk with you, O noble priests,' I said.

Before they could think up a good answer, I was inside.

The temple was a small one built against the base of the pyramid. I hoped I wasn't breaking too many taboos by going in, I wasn't stopped, so it looked all right. The temple was a single room with a murky-looking pool at one end. Sloshing in the pool was an ancient reptile who clearly was one of the leaders. I waddled toward him and he gave me a cold and fishy eye, then growled something.

The MT whispered into my ear, 'Just what in the name of the thirteenth sin are you doing here?'

I drew up my scaly figure in a noble gesture and pointed toward the ceiling. 'I come from your ancestors to help you. I am here to restore the Holy Waters.'

This raised a buzz of conversation behind me, but got no rise out of the chief. He sank slowly into the water until only his eyes were showing. I could almost hear the wheels turning behind that moss-covered forehead. Then he lunged up and pointed a dripping finger at me.

'You are a liar! You are no ancestor of ours! We will—'

'Stop!' I thundered before he got so far in that he couldn't back out. 'I said your ancestors sent me as emissary – I am not one of your ancestors. Do not try to harm me or the wrath of those who have Passed On will turn against you.'

When I said this; I turned to jab a claw at the other priests, using the motion to cover my flicking a coin grenade toward them. It blew a nice hole in the floor with a great show of noise and smoke.

The First Lizard knew I was talking sense then and immediately called a meeting of the shamans. It, of course, took place in the public bathtub and I had to join them there. We jawed and gurgled for about an hour and settled all the major points.

I found out that they were new priests; the previous ones had all been boiled for letting the Holy Waters cease. I explained that I was there only to help them restore the flow of the waters. They bought this, tentatively, and we all heaved out of the tub and trickled muddy paths across the floor. There was a bolted and guarded door that led into the pyramid proper. While it was being opened, the First Lizard turned to me.

'Undoubtedly you know of the rule,' he said. 'Because the old priests did pry and peer, it was ordered henceforth that only the blind could enter the Holy of Holies.' I'd swear he was smiling, if thirty teeth peeking out of what looked like a crack in an old suitcase can be called smiling.

He was also signaling to him an underpriest who carried a brazier of charcoal complete with red-hot irons. All I could do was stand and watch as he stirred up the coals, pulled out the ruddiest iron and turned toward me. He was just drawing a bead on my right eyeball when my brain got back in gear.

'Of course,' I said, 'blinding is only right. But in my case you will have to blind me before I leave the Holy of Holies, not now. I need my eyes to see and mend the Fount of Holy Waters. Once the waters flow again, I will laugh as I hurl myself on the burning iron.'

He took a good thirty seconds to think it over and had to agree with me. The local torturer sniffled a bit and threw a little more charcoal on the fire. The gate crashed open and I stalked through; then it banged to behind me and I was alone in the dark.

But not for long – there was a shuffling nearby and I took a chance and turned on my flash. Three priests were groping toward me, their eye-sockets red pits of burned flesh. They knew what I wanted and led the way without a word.

A crumbling and cracked stone stairway brought us up to a solid metal doorway labeled in archaic script MARK III BEACON – AUTHORIZED PERSONNEL ONLY. The trusting builders counted on the sign to do the whole job, for there wasn't a trace of a lock on the door. One lizard merely turned the handle and we were inside the beacon.

I unzipped the front of my camouflage suit and pulled out the blueprints. With the faithful priests stumbling after me, I located the control room and turned on the lights. There was a residue of charge in the emergency batteries, just enough to give a dim light. The meters and indicators looked to be in good shape; if anything, unexpectedly bright from constant polishing.

I checked the readings carefully and found just what I had suspected. One of the eager lizards had managed to open a circuit box and had polished the switches inside. While doing this, he had thrown one of the switches and that had caused the trouble.

Rather, that had *started* the trouble. It wasn't going to be ended by just reversing the water-valve switch. This valve was supposed to be used only for repairs, after the pile had been damped. When the water was cut off with the pile in operation, it had started to overheat and the automatic safeties had dumped the charge down the pit.

I could start the water again easily enough, but there was no fuel left in the reactor.

I wasn't going to play with the fuel problem at all. It would be far easier to install a new power plant. I had one in the ship that was about a tenth the size of the ancient bucket of bolts and produced at least four times the power. Before I sent for it, I checked over the rest of the beacon. In 2000 years, there should be *some* sign of wear.

The old boys had built well, I'll give them credit for that. Ninety per cent of the machinery had no moving parts and had suffered no wear whatever. Other parts they had beefed up, figuring they would wear, but slowly. The water-feed pipe from the roof, for example. The pipe walls were at least three meters thick – and the pipe opening itself no bigger than my head. There were some things I could do, though, and I made a list of parts.

The parts, the new power plant and a few other odds and ends were chuted into a neat pile on the ship. I checked all the parts by screen before they were loaded in a metal crate. In the darkest hour before dawn, the heavy-duty Eye dropped the crate outside the temple and darted away without being seen.

I watched the priests through the pryeye while they tried to open it. When they had given up, I boomed orders at them through a speaker in the crate. They spent most of the day sweating the heavy box up through the narrow temple stairs and I enjoyed a good sleep. It was resting inside the beacon door when I woke up.

The repairs didn't take long, though there was plenty of groaning from the blind lizards when they heard me ripping the wall open to get at the power leads. I even hooked a gadget to the water pipe so their Holy Waters would have the usual refreshing radioactivity when they started flowing again. The moment this was all finished, I did the job they were waiting for.

I threw the switch that started the water flowing again.

There were a few minutes while the water began to gurgle down through the dry pipe. Then a roar came from outside the pyramid that must have shaken its stone walls. Shaking my hands once over my head, I went down for the eye-burning ceremony.

The blind lizards were waiting for me by the door and looked even unhappier than usual. When I tried the door, I found out why – it was bolted and barred from the other side.

'It has been decided,' a lizard said, 'that you shall remain here forever and tend the Holy Waters. We will stay with you and serve your every need.'

A delightful prospect, eternity spent in a locked beacon with three blind lizards. In spite of their hospitality, I couldn't accept.

'What – you dare interfere with the messenger of your ancestors!' I had the speaker on full volume and the vibration almost shook my head off.

The lizards cringed and I set my Solar for a narrow beam and ran it around the door jamb. There was a great crunching and banging from the junk piled against it, and then the door swung free. I threw it open. Before they could protest, I had pushed the priests out through it.

The rest of their clan showed up at the foot of the stairs

and made a great ruckus while I finished welding the door shut. Running through the crowd, I faced up to the First Lizard in his tub. He sank slowly beneath the surface.

'What lack of courtesy!' I shouted. He made little bubbles in the water. 'The ancestors are annoyed and have decided to forbid entrance to the Inner Temple forever; though, out of kindness, they will let the waters flow. Now I must return – on with the ceremony!'

The torture-master was too frightened to move, so I grabbed out his hot iron. A touch on the side of my face dropped a steel plate over my eyes, under the plastiskin. Then I jammed the iron hard into my phony eye-sockets and the plastic gave off an authentic odor.

A cry went up from the crowd as I dropped the iron and staggered in blind circles. I must admit it went off pretty well.

Before they could get any more bright ideas, I threw the switch and my plastic pterodactyl sailed in through the door. I couldn't see it, of couse, but I knew it had arrived when the grapples in the claws latched onto the steel plates on my shoulders.

I had got turned around after the eye-burning and my flying beast hooked onto me backward. I had meant to sail out bravely, blind eyes facing into the sunset; instead, I faced the crowd as I soared away, so I made the most of a bad situation and threw them a snappy military salute. Then I was out in the fresh air and away.

When I lifted the plate and poked holes in the seared plastic, I could see the pyramid growing smaller behind me, water gushing out of the base and a happy crowd of reptiles sporting in its radioactive rush. I counted off on my talons to see if I had forgotten anything.

One: The beacon was repaired.

Two: The door was sealed, so there should be no more sabotage, accidental or deliberate.

Three: The priests should be satisfied. The water was running again, my eyes had been duly burned out, and they were back in business. Which added up to—

Four: The fact that they would probably let another repairman in, under the same conditions, if the beacon conked out again. At least I had done nothing, like butchering a few of them, that would make them antagonistic toward future ancestral messengers.

I stripped off my tattered lizard suit back in the ship, very glad that it would be some other repairman who'd get the job.

Man may some day outgrow his interest in war, but don't hold your breath. The combative urge was such a strong factor in scaling the evolutionary ladder that it cannot be easily put aside; and while the idea of war may terrify us and disgust us, the prehistoric bodies we wear still react enthusiastically when the drums roll and the cannons rumble by. As witness our present situation – we watch with fascinated interest as all sorts of ingenious and dedicated people work up the weapons that can, if That Button ever gets pushed, wipe us all from this planet.

Should this not happen, man will very likely cheerfully export his wars to the rest of the galaxy. If the alien races encountered are not warlike enough to fight back ... too bad for them. And if there aren't enough aliens around to fight, man will just have to fight his oldest enemy. Himself. Of course, his companions, the robots, will fight as well. And it's all too clear that in some ways a robot would be a perfect soldier – less destructible, more efficient at destruction ... and, of course, you can build in the killer-instinct. ...

SURVIVAL PLANET

'But this war was finished years before I was born! How can one robot torpedo – fired that long ago – still be of any interest?'

Dall the Younger was overly persistent – it was extremely lucky for him that Ship-Commander Lian Stane, both by temperament and experience, had a tremendous reserve of patience.

'It has been fifty years since the Greater Slavocracy was defeated – but that doesn't mean eliminated,' Commander Stane said. He looked through the viewport of the ship, seeing ghostlike against the stars the pattern of the empire they had fought so long to destroy. 'The Slavocracy expanded unchecked for over a thousand years. Its military defeat didn't finish it, just made the separate worlds accessible to us. We are still in the middle of that reconstruction, guiding them away from a slave economy.'

'That I know *all* about,' Dall the Younger broke in with a weary sigh. 'I've been working on the planets since I came into the force. But what has that got to do with the Mosaic torpedo that we're tracking? There must have been a billion of them made and fired during the war. How can a single one be of interest this much later?'

'If you had read the tech reports,' Stane said, pointing to the thumb-thick folder on the chart table, 'you would know all about it.' This advice was the closest the Commander had ever come to censure. Dall the Younger had the good grace to flush slightly and listen with applied attention.

'The Mosaic torpedo is a weapon of space war, in reality a robot-controlled spaceship. Once directed it seeks out its target, defends itself if necessary, then destroys itself and the ship it has been launched against by starting the uncontrollable cycle of binding-energy breakdown.'

'I never realized that they were robot-operated,' Dall said. 'I thought robots had an ingrained resistance to killing people?'

'In-*built* rather than ingrained would be more accurate,' Stane said judiciously. 'Robotic brains are just highly developed machines with no inherent moral sense. That is added afterwards. It has been a long time since we built man-shaped robots with human-type brains. This is the age of the specialist, and robots can specialize far better than men ever could. The Mosaic torpedo brains have no moral sense – if anything they are psychotic, overwhelmed by a death wish. Though there are, of course, controls on how much they can kill. All the torpedoes ever used by either side had mass detectors to defuse them when they approached any object with planetary mass, since the reaction started by a torpedo could just as easily destroy a world as a ship. You can understand our interest when in the last months of the war, we picked up a torpedo fused *only* to detonate a planet. All the data from its brain was filed and recently interpreted. The torpedo was aimed at the fourth planet of the star we are approaching now.'

'Anything on the record about this planet?' Dall asked.

'Nothing. It is an unexplored system – at least as far as our records are concerned. But the Greater Slavocracy knew enough about this planet to want to destroy it. We are here to find out why.'

Dall the Younger furrowed his brow, chewing at the idea. 'Is that the only reason?' he finally asked. 'Since we stopped them from wiping out this planet, that would be the end of it, I should think.'

'It's thinking like that that shows why you are the low-ranker on this ship,' Gunner Arnild snapped as he came in. Arnild had managed to grow old in a very short-lived service, losing in the process, his patience for everything except his computers and guns. 'Shall I suggest some of the possibilities that have occurred even to me? Firstly – any enemy of the Slavocracy could be a friend of ours. Or conversely, there may be an enemy here that threatens the entire human race, and we may need to set off a Mosaic ourselves to finish the job the Slavers started. Then again, the Slavers may have had something here – like a research center – that they would rather have destroyed than let us see. Wouldn't you say that any one of these would make the planet worth investigating?'

'We shall be in the atmosphere within twenty hours,' Dall said as he vanished through the lower hatch. 'I have to check the lubrication on the drive gears.'

'You're too easy on the kid,' Gunner Arnild said, staring moodily at the approaching star, already dimmed by the forward filters.

'And you're too hard,' Stane told him. 'So I guess it evens out. You forget he never fought the Slavers.'

Skimming the outer edges of the atmosphere of the fourth planet, the scout ship hurled itself through the measured length of a helical orbit, then fled back into the safety of space while the ship's robot brain digested and made copies of the camera and detector instrument recordings. The duplicates were stored in a message torp, and only when the torp had started back to base did Commander Stane bother personally to examine the results of their survey.

'We're dispensable now,' he said, relaxing. 'So the best thing we can do is to drop down and see what we can stir up.' Arnild grunted agreement, his index fingers unconsciously pressing invisible triggers. They leaned over the graphs and photographs spread out on the table. Dall peered between their shoulders and flipped through the photographs they tossed aside. He was first to speak.

'Nothing much there, really. Plenty of water, a big island continent – and not much else.'

'Nothing else is detectable,' Stane added, ticking off the graphs one by one. 'No detectable radiation, no large masses of metal either above or below ground, no stored energy. No reason for us to be here.'

'But we are,' Arnild growled testily. 'So let's touch down and find out more first hand. Here's a good spot,' he tapped a photograph, then pushed it into the enlarger. 'Could be a primitive hut city, people walking around, smoke.'

'Those could be sheep in the fields,' Dall broke in eagerly. 'And boats pulled up on the shore. We'll find out something there.'

'I'm sure we will,' Commander Stane said. 'Strap in for landing.'

Lightly and soundlessly the ship fell out of the sky, curving in a gentle arc that terminated at the edge of a grove of tall trees, on a hill above the city. The motors whined to a stop and the ship was silent.

'Report positive on the atmosphere,' Dall said, checking off the analyzer dials.

'Stay at the guns, Arnild,' Commander Stane said. 'Keep us covered, but don't shoot unless I tell you to.'

'Or unless you're dead,' Arnild said with complete lack of emotion.

'Or unless I'm dead,' Stane answered him, in the same toneless voice. 'In which case you will assume command.'

He and Dall buckled on planet kits, cycled through the lock and sealed it behind them. The air was soft and pleasantly warm, filled with the freshness of growing plants.

'Really smells good after that canned stuff,' Dall said.

'You have a great capacity for stating the obvious.' Arnild's voice rasped even more than usual when heard through the bone conductor phones. 'Can you see what's going on in the village?'

Dall fumbled his binoculars out. Commander Stane had been using his since they left the ship. 'Nothing moving,' Stane said. 'Send an Eye down there.'

The Eye whooshed away from the ship and they could follow its slow swing through the village below. There were about a hundred huts, simple pole-and-thatch affairs, and the Eye carefully investigated every one.

'No one there,' Arnild said, as he watched the monitor

screen. 'The animals are gone too, the ones from the aerial pic.'

'The people *can't* have vanished,' Dall said. 'There are empty fields in every direction, completely without cover. And I can see smoke from their fires.'

'The smoke's there, the people aren't,' Arnild said testily. 'Walk down and look for yourself.'

The Eye lifted up from the village and drifted back towards the ship. It swung around the trees and came to a sudden stop in mid-air.

'Hold it!' Arnild's voice snapped in their ears. 'The huts are empty. But there's someone in the tree you're standing next to. About ten metres over your heads!'

Both men controlled a natural reaction to look up. They moved out a bit, where they would be safe from anything dropped from above.

'Far enough,' Arnild said. 'I'm shifting the Eye for a better look.' They could hear the faint drone of the Eye's motors as it changed position.

'It's a girl. Wearing some kind of fur outfit. No weapons that I can see, but some kind of a pouch hanging from her waist. She's just clutching onto the tree with her eyes closed. Looks like she's afraid of falling.'

The men on the ground could see her dimly now a huddled shape against the straight trunk.

'Don't bring the Eye any closer,' Commander Stane said. 'But turn the speaker on. Hook my phone into the circuit.'

'You're plugged in.'

'*We are friends ... Come down ... We will not hurt you.*' The words boomed down from the floating speaker above their heads.

'She heard it, but maybe she can't understand Speranto,' Arnild said. 'She just hugged the tree harder while you were talking.'

Commander Stane had had a good command of Slaver during the war, he groped in his memory for the words, doing a quick translation. He repeated the same phrase, only this time in the tongue of their defeated enemies.

'That did something, Commander,' Arnild reported. 'She jumped so hard she almost fell off. Then scooted up a couple of branches higher before she grabbed on again.'

'Let me get her down, sir,' Dall asked. 'I'll take some rope and climb up after her. It's the only way. Like getting a cat out of a tree.'

Stane pushed the thought around. 'It looks like the best answer,' he finally said. 'Get the light-weight 200-metre line and the climbing irons out of the ship. Don't take too long, it'll be getting dark soon.'

The irons chunked into the wood and Dall climbed carefully up to the lower limbs. Above him the girl stirred and he had a quick glimpse of the white patch of her face as she looked down at him. He started climbing again until Arnild's voice snapped at him.

'Hold it! She's climbing higher. Staying above you.'

'What'll I do, Commander?' Dall asked, settling himself in the fork of one of the big branches. He felt exhilarated by the climb, his skin tingling slightly with sweat. He snapped open his collar and breathed deeply.

'Keep going. She can't climb any higher than the top of the tree.'

The climbing was easier now, the branches smaller and closer together. He went slowly so as not to frighten the girl into a misstep. The ground was out of sight, far below. They were alone in their own world of leaves and swaying boughs, the silver tube of the hovering Eye the only reminder of the watchers from the ship. Dall stopped to tie a loop in the end of the rope, doing it carefully so the knot would hold. For the first time since they had started on this mission he felt as if he was doing a full part. The two old warhorses weren't bad shipmates, but they oppressed him with the years of their experience. But this was something *he* could do best and he whistled softly through his teeth with the thought.

It would have been possible for the girl to have climbed higher, the branches could have held her weight. But for some reason she had retreated out along a branch. Another, close to it, made a perfect handhold, and he shuffled slowly after her.

'No reason to be afraid,' he said cheerfully, and smiled. 'Just want to get you down safely and back to your friends. Why don't you grab onto this rope?'

The girl just shuddered and backed away. She was young and good to look at, dressed only in a short, fur kilt. Her hair was long, but had been combed and caught back of her head with a thong. The only thing that appeared alien about her was her fear. As he came closer he could see she was drenched with it. Her legs and arms shook with a steady vibration. Her teeth were clamped into her whitened lips and a thin trickle of blood reached to her chin. He hadn't thought it possible that human eyes could have stared so widely, or have been so filled with desperation.

'You don't have to be afraid,' he repeated, stopping just out of reach. The branch was thin and springy. If he tried to grab her they might both be bounced off it. He didn't want any accidents to happen now. Slowly pulling the rope from the coil, Dall tied it about his waist, then made a loop around the next branch. Out of the corner of his eye he saw the girl stir and look around wildly.

'Friends!' he said, trying to calm her. He translated it into Slaver, she had seemed to understand that before '*No'r venn!*'

Her mouth opened wide and her legs contracted. The scream was terrible and more like a tortured animal's cry than a human voice. It confused him and he made a desperate grab. It was too late.

She didn't fall. With all her strength she hurled herself from the limb, jumping towards the certain death she preferred to his touch. For a heartbeat she seemed to hang, contorted and fear-crazed, at the apex of her leap, before gravity clutched hold and pulled her crashing down through the leaves. Then Dall was falling too, grabbing for non-existent handholds.

The safety line he had tied held fast. In a half-daze he worked his way back to the trunk and fumbled loose the knots. With quivering precision he made his way back to the ground. It took a long time and a blanket was drawn over the deformed thing in the grass before he reached it. He didn't have to ask if she was dead.

'I tried to stop her. I did my best.' There was a slight touch of shrillness to Dall's voice.

'Of course,' Commander Stane told him, as he spread out the contents of the girl's waist pouch. 'We were watching with the Eye. There was no way to stop her when she decided to jump.'

'No need to talk Slaver to her either—' Arnild said, coming out of the ship. He was going to add something, but he caught Commander Stane's direct look and shut his mouth. Dall saw it too.

'I forgot!' the young man said, looking back and forth at their expressionless faces. 'I just remembered she had understood Slaver. I didn't think it would frighten her. It was a mistake maybe, but anyone can make a mistake! I didn't want her to die . . .'

He clamped his trembling jaws shut with an effort, and turned away.

'You better get some food started,' Commander Stane told him. As soon as the port had closed he pointed to the girl's body. 'Bury her under the trees, I'll help you.'

It was a brief meal, none of them were very hungry. Stane sat at the chart table afterward pushing the hard green fruit around with his forefinger. 'This is what she was doing in the tree – why she couldn't pull the vanishing act like the others. Picking fruit. She had nothing else in the pouch. Our landing next to the tree and trapping her was pure accident.' He glanced at Dall's face, then turned quickly away.

'It's too dark to see now, do we wait for morning?' Arnild asked. He had a hand gun disassembled on the table, adjusting and oiling the parts.

Commander Stane nodded. 'It can't do any harm – and it's better than stumbling around in the dark. Leave an Eye with an infra-red projector and filter over the village and make a recording. Maybe we can find out where they all went.'

'I'll stay at the Eye controls,' Dall said suddenly. 'I'm not ... sleepy. I might find something out.'

The Commander hesitated for a moment, then agreed. 'Wake me if you see anything. Otherwise, get us up at dawn.'

The night was quiet and nothing moved in the silent village of huts. At first light Commander Stane and Dall walked down the hill, an Eye floating ahead to cover them. Arnild stayed behind in the locked ship, at the controls.

'Over this way, sir,' Dall said. 'Something I found during the night when I was making sweeps with the Eye.'

The pit edges had been softened and rounded by the weather, large trees grew on the slopes. At the bottom, projecting from a pool of water, were the remains of rusted machinery.

'I think they're excavation machines,' Dall said. 'Though it's hard to tell, they've been down there so long.'

The Eye dropped down to the bottom of the pit and nosed close to the wreckage. It sank below the water and emerged after a minute, trailing a wet stream.

'Digging machines, all right,' Arnild reported. 'Some of them turned over and half buried, like they fell in the hole. And all of them Slaver built.'

Commander Stane looked up intently. 'Are you sure?' he asked.

'Sure as I can read a label.'

'Let's get on to the village,' the Commander said, chewing thoughtfully at the inside of his cheek.

Dall the Younger discovered where the villagers had gone. It was really no secret, they found out in the first hut they entered. The floor was made of pounded dirt, with a circle of rocks for a fireplace. All the other contents were of the simplest and crudest. Heavy, unfired clay pots, untanned furs, some eating utensils chipped out of hard wood. Dall was poking through a heap of woven mats behind the fireplace when he found the hole.

'Over here, sir!' he called.

The opening was almost a meter in diameter and sank into the ground at an easy angle. The floor of the tunnel was beaten as hard as the floor of the hut.

'They must be hiding out in there,' Commander Stane said. 'Flash a light down and see how deep it is.'

There was no way to tell. The hole was really a smooth walled tunnel that turned at a sharp angle five meters inside the entrance. The Eye swooped down and hung, humming, above the opening.

'I took a look in some of the other huts,' Arnild said from the ship. 'The Eye found a hole like this in every one of them. Want me to take a look inside?'

'Yes, but take it slowly,' Commander Stane told him. 'If there are people hiding down there we don't want to frighten them more. Drift down and pull back if you find anything.'

The humming died as the Eye floated down the tunnel and out of sight.

'Joined another tunnel,' Arnild reported. 'And now another junction. Getting confused ... don't know if I can get it back the way I sent it in.'

'The Eye is expendable,' the Commander told him. 'Keep going.'

'Must be dense rock around ... signal is getting weaker and I have a job holding control. A bigger cavern of some sort – *wait*! There's someone! Caught a look at a man going into one of the side tunnels.'

'Follow him,' Stane said.

'Not easy,' Arnild said after a moment's silence. 'Looks like a dead end. A rock of some kind blocking the tunnel. He must have rolled it back and blocked the passage after he went by. I'll back out ... *Blast!*'

'What's wrong?'

'Another rock behind the Eye – they've got it trapped in that hunk of tunnel. Now the screen's dead, and all I can get is an out-of-operation signal!' Arnild sounded exasperated and angry.

'Very neat,' Commander Stane said. 'They lured it in, trapped it – then probably collapsed the roof of the tunnel. These people are very suspicious of strangers and seem to have a certain efficiency at getting rid of them.'

'But *why*?' Dall asked, frankly puzzled, looking around at the crude construction of the hut. 'What do these people have that the Slavers could have wanted so badly? It's obvious that the Slavers put a lot of time and effort into trying to dig down there. Did they ever find what they were looking for? Did they try to destroy this planet because they *had* found it – or *hadn't* found it?'

'I wish I knew,' Commander Stane said glumly. 'It would make my job a lot easier. We'll get a complete report off to HQ – maybe they have some ideas.'

On the way back to the ship they noticed the fresh dirt in the grove of trees. There was a raw empty hole where the girl had been buried. The ground had been torn apart and hurled in every direction. There were slash marks on the trunks of the trees, made by sharp blades ... or giant claws. Something or somebody had come for the girl, dug up her body and vented a burning rage on the ground and the trees. A crushed trail led to an opening between the roofs of one of the trees. It slanted back and down, its dark mouth as enigmatic and mysterious as the other tunnels.

Before they retired that night, Commander Stane made a double check that the ports were locked and all the alarm circuits activated. He went to bed but didn't sleep. The answer to the problem seemed tantalizingly obvious, hovering just outside his reach. There seemed to be enough facts here to draw a conclusion from. But what? He drifted into a fitful doze without finding the answer.

When he awoke the cabin was still dark, and he had the feeling something was terribly wrong. What had awakened him? He groped in his sleep-filled memories. A sigh. A rush of air. It could have been the cycling of the air lock. Fighting down the sudden fear he snapped on the lights and pulled his gun from the bedside rack. Arnild appeared, yawning and blinking in the doorway.

'What's going on?' he asked.

'Get Dall – I think someone came into the ship.'

'Gone out is more like it,' Arnild snuffed. 'Dall's not in his bunk.'

'What!'

He ran to the control room. The alarm circuit had been turned off. There was a piece of paper on the control console. The Commander grabbed it up and read the single word written on it. He gaped as comprehension struck him, then crushed the paper in his convulsive fist.

'The fool!' he shouted. 'The damned young fool! Break out an Eye. No, two! I'll work the duplicate controls!'

'But what's happened?' Arnild gaped. 'What's young Dall done?'

'Gone underground. Into the tunnels. We have to stop him!'

Dall was nowhere in sight, but the lip of the tunnel under the trees was freshly crumbled.

'I'll take an Eye down there,' Commander Stane said. 'You take another one down the next nearest entrance. Use the speakers. Tell them that we are friends, in Slaver.'

'But – you saw what reaction the girl had when Dall told her that.' Arnild was puzzled, confused.

'I know what happened,' Stane snapped. 'But what other choice do we have? Now get on with it!'

Arnild started to ask another question, but the huddled intensity of the Commander at the controls changed his mind. He sent his own Eye rocketing towards the village.

If the people hiding in the maze of tunnels heard the message, they certainly didn't believe it. One Eye was trapped in a dead-end tunnel when the opening behind it suddenly filled with soft dirt. Commander Stane tried nosing the machine through the dirt, but it was firmly trapped and held. He could hear thumpings and digging as more dirt was piled on top.

Arnild's Eye found a large underground chamber, filled with huddled and frightened sheep. There were none of the natives there. On the way out of this cavern the Eye was trapped under a fall of rocks.

In the end, Commander Stane admitted defeat. 'It's up to them now, we can't change the end one way or another.'

'Something moving in the grove of trees, Commander,' Arnild said sharply. 'Caught it on the detector, but it's gone now.'

They went out hesitantly with their guns pointed, under a reddened dawn sky. They went, half-knowing what they would find, but fearful to admit it aloud while they could still hope.

Of course there was no hope. Dall the Younger's body lay near the tunnel mouth, out of which it had been pushed. The red dawn glinted from red blood. He had died terribly.

'They're fiends! Animals!' Arnild shouted. 'To do that to a man who only wanted to help them. Broke his arms and legs, scratched away most of his skin. His face – nothing left...' The aging gunner choked out a sound that was half gasp, half sob. 'They ought to be bombed out, blown up! Like the Slavers started...' He met the Commander's burning stare and fell silent.

'That's probably just how the Slavers felt,' Stane said. 'Don't you understand what happened here?'

Arnild shook his head dumbly.

'Dall had a glimpse of the truth. Only he thought it was possible to change things. But at least he knew what the danger was. He went because he felt guilty for the girl's death. That was why he left the note with the word *slaves* on it, in case he didn't come back.'

'It's really quite simple,' he said wearily, leaning back against a tree. 'Only we were looking for something more complex and technical. When it wasn't really a physical problem, but a social one we were facing. This was a Slaver planet, set up and organized by the Slavers to fit their special needs.'

'What?' Arnild asked, still confused.

'Slaves. They were constantly expanding, and you know that their style of warfare was expensive on manpower. They needed steady sources of supply and must have created them. This planet was one answer. Made to order in a way. A single, lightly forested continent, with few places for the people to hide when the slave ships came. They planted a nucleus, gave the people simple and sufficient sources of food, but absolutely no technology. Then they went away to let them breed. Every few years they would come back, take as many slaves as they needed, and leave the others to replenish the stock. Only they reckoned without one thing.'

Arnild's numbness was wearing off. He understood now.

'The adaptability of mankind,' he said.

'Of course. The ability – given enough time – to adapt to almost any extreme of environment. This is a perfect example. A cut-off population with no history, no written language – just the desire to survive. Every few years unspeakable creatures drop out of the sky and steal their children. They try running away, but there is no place to run. They build boats, but there is no place to sail to. Nothing works . . .'

'Until one bright boy digs a hole, covers it up and hides his family in it. And finds out it works.'

'The beginning,' Commander Stane nodded. 'The idea spreads, the tunnels get deeper and more elaborate when the Slavers try to dig them out. Until the slaves finally win. This was probably the first planet to rebel successfully against the Greater Slavocracy. They couldn't be dug out. Poison gas would just kill them and they had no value dead. Machines sent after them were trapped like our Eyes. And men who were foolish enough to go down . . .' He couldn't finish the sentence, Dall's body was stronger evidence than words could ever be.

'But the hatred?' Arnild asked. 'The way the girl killed herself rather than be taken.'

'The tunnels became a religion,' Stane told him. 'They had to be, to be kept in operation and repair during the long gap of years between visits by the Slavers. The children had to be taught that the demons come from the skies and salvation lies below. The opposite of the old Earth religions. Hatred and fear were implanted so everyone, no matter how young, would know what to do if a ship appeared. There must be entrances everywhere. Seconds after a ship is sighted the population can vanish underground. They knew we were Slavers since only demons come from the sky.

'Dall must have guessed part of this. Only he thought he could reason with them, explain that the Slavers were gone and that they didn't have to hide any more. That good men come from the skies. But that's heresy, and by itself would be enough to get him killed. If they ever bothered to listen.'

They were gentle when they carried Dall the Younger back to his ship.

'It'll be a job trying to convince these people of the truth.' They paused for a moment to rest. 'I still don't understand though, why the Slavers wanted to blow the planet up.'

'There too, we were looking for too complex a motive,' Commander Stane said. 'Why does a conquering army blow up buildings and destroy monuments when it is forced to retreat? Just frustration and anger, old human emotions. If I can't have it, you can't either. This planet must have annoyed the Slavers for years. A successful rebellion that they couldn't put down. They kept trying to capture the rebels since they were incapable of admitting defeat at the hands of slaves. When they knew their war was lost, destruction of this planet was a happy vent for their emotions. I noticed you feeling the same way yourself when you saw Dall's body. It's a human reaction.'

They were both old soldiers, so they didn't show their emotions too much when they put Dall's corpse into the special chamber and readied the ship for takeoff.

But they were old men as well, much older since they had come to this planet, and they moved now with old men's stiffness.

There aren't many really talented inventors or perfectionists in the human population, but it doesn't take many to keep things humming right along. The Wright brothers made the first powered flight in 1903, and less than forty-five years later airplanes were in production with a wingspan greater than the total distance of this first flight, not to mention the size of the plane. *Homo sapiens* is a born improver. Everything keeps getting bigger and bigger and better and better.

This applies to war too. Space wars only give an illusion of being bigger and better than other wars, no doubt due to the gigantic size of the field of action. But they can be frustrating because so few people can be involved and blown up at the same time. Sooner or later, in spite of all the forces of enlightenment, war will return to battered old Mother Earth. Different groups will find important things to differ about, and very logically, differences of opinion will be settled in the tried and true manner – by combat.

Of course the robots will help since by this time, after so much training, they will be getting very good at the game themselves. This robot participation will take away a great amount of the pleasure gained from hand-to-hand combat, but a perfecting trend cannot be stopped. As long as one side gets a little bit ahead, the other side has to rush to catch up.

Until in the end we will have global warfare of a truly majestic sort, where the entire surface of the planet, the air and the seas will be a single gigantic battleground. . . .

WAR WITH THE ROBOTS

Only the slightest vibration could be felt through the floor of the hurtling monorail car. There was no sensation of motion since the rushing tunnel walls could not be seen through the windowless sides. The riders, all of them in neatly pressed uniforms with buttons and decorations shining, swayed slightly in their seats on the turns, wrapped in their own thoughts and mumbled conversations. Above them, thousands of feet of solid rock sealed them off from the war. At an effortless one-hundred and fifty miles an hour the car rushed General Pere and his staff to their battle stations.

When the alarm screamed the driver clamped the brakes full on and reversed his motors. There was not enough time. At full speed the metal bullet tore into the barrier of rocks and dirt that blocked the tunnel. Steel plates crushed and crumpled as the car slammed to a halt. All the lights went out; and in the empty silence that followed the ear-shattering clamor of the crash only a faint moaning could be heard.

General Pere pushed himself up from the chair, shaking his head in an effort to clear it, and snapped on his flash. The beam nervously danced the length of the car, gleaming on settling dust motes and lighting up the frightened white faces of his staff.

'Casualty report, verbal,' he told his adjutant, his voice pitched low so that no quaver might be heard. It is not easy to be a general when you are only nineteen years old. Pere forced himself to stand still while the metal back of the adjutant robot moved swiftly up the aisle.

The seats were well anchored and faced to the rear, so it

was hopeful that there would not be too many casualties. Behind the backs of the last chairs was a rubble of dirt that had burst in through the destroyed nose. The driver was undoubtedly dead under it, which was all for the best. It saved the trouble of a court-martial.

'One killed, one missing in action, one wounded, total active strength of unit now seventeen.' The adjutant dropped the salute and stood at attention, waiting further orders. General Pere nervously chewed his lip.

Missing-in-action meant the driver. Presumed dead, damn well dead. The 'one killed' was the new captain from Interceptor Control, who had had the bad luck to be leaning out of his chair at the time of the accident. His neck had been cracked on the edge of the chair and his head now hung down at a sickening angle. The moaning must be the wounded man, he had better check on that first. He stamped down the aisle and shined his light on the sallow, sweatbeaded face of Colonel Zen.

'My arm, sir,' the Colonel gasped. 'I was reaching out when we crashed, my arm whipped back and hit the metal edge. Broken I think. The pain . . .'

'That's enough, Colonel,' Pere said. A little too loudly, because the man's fear was beginning to touch him too. There were footsteps in the aisle and his second-in-command, General Natia, joined him.

'You've had the standard first-aid course, General,' Pere said. 'Bandage this man and then report to me.'

'Yes, sir,' General Natia said, her voice echoing that same note of fear.

Damn all, Pere thought, *she should know that's no way for a general to act. We can't let the troops know we're afraid – even if we are.* He made no allowance for the fact that General Natia was a woman, and just eighteen.

Once his staff had been attended to he turned his mind to the problems at hand. Some of the tension eased as he sorted out all the factors. Problem solving was his speciality, and he had been selected for it before birth. Gene analysis had chosen the best DNA chain from his parents' sperm-and-ovum bank. This, and subsequent training, had fitted him perfectly for command. With the instantaneous reflexes of youth, he was a formidable opponent on the battlefield and looked forward to a successful career of at least four or five years before retirement.

For a man who would soon be directing a global conflict this problem was childishly simple.

'Communications?' he snapped, and pointed his finger at the Signal Corps Major. There was an automatic authority in his voice now, in marked contrast to his boyish crewcut and freckles.

'None, sir,' the officer said, saluting. 'Whatever blocked the tunnel knocked out the land lines as well. I've tried with the field phone but the wires are dead.'

'Does anyone know how far we are from HQ?' he asked, raising his voice so that all the officers in the car could hear him.

'I'll have it ... in a second, sir,' one of them said, a grey-haired colonel from Computer Corps. He was moving the scale on his pocket slide rule, blinking intently in the light of his flash. 'Don't know how long this tunnel is – or the exact location of HQ. But I have made the run before, and the total elapsed time is usually a few minutes over three hours. Figuring the time to the accident, our speed, allowing for deceleration....' His voice trailed off into a mumble and Pere waited impatiently, but unmoving. He needed this information before he could make his next move.

'Between forty and sixty miles to HQ, sir. And those are the outside figures, I'd say it's very close to fifty ...'

'That's good enough. I want two volunteers, you and you. Get up in the nose there and see if you can't dig a hole through that rubble. We're going to try to get through and continue on foot. We'll be needed at HQ if the Enemy is able to hit this close.'

This last was added for the sake of his staff's morale, the training courses had recommended the human touch whenever possible. Particularly in unusual situations. And this was an unusual, though not very promising way for his first command to begin. He scowled unhappily into the darkness. It took an effort to keep his feelings from his voice as he issued orders to assemble the food stores and water. When this was done he sent his adjutant to relieve the two men who were digging into the dirt barricade. One robot was worth ten men – not to say two – at this kind of labor.

It took almost twelve hours to penetrate the barrier, and they were all completely exhausted before it was through. The adjutant did all the digging, and they rotated shifts in carrying away the rubble that he cleared. There had been some minor falls of dirt and rock that in their haste they ignored, until a major fall at the work face had completely buried the robot. They dug until they reached its feet and Pere had lengths of the now useless tunnel signal wire tied around the robot's ankles. It wasn't until they had added loops of wire so that they could all pull together that the adjutant had been dragged from his near grave. After that work slowed, since they had to unbolt the chairs from the car and use them to shore up the roof. All things considered, twelve hours was good time for penetration of the barrier.

Once they were through General Pere allowed them a half-hour break. They sipped at their water bottles and collapsed wearily on both sides of the central track. Pride and position would not allow Pere to rest; he paced ahead to see if the tunnel was clear, his adjutant beside him.

'How many hours left in your battery?' Pere asked. 'At maximum output.'

'Over three hundred.'

'Then start running. If you come to any other falls begin clearing them away and we'll catch up with you. If you get through without any trouble have them send a car for us. It will save some time.'

The robot saluted and was gone, his running steps thudding away in the distance. Pere looked at the glowing dial of his watch and announced the end of the break.

Walking, with the single light twinkling ahead, soon took on a dream-like quality that numbed their responses. They went on this way, with short breaks every hour, for almost eight hours. When they began to drop out, asleep on their feet, Pere reluctantly ordered a stop. He forced them to eat first, then allowed them only four hours' sleep before he forcefully shook them to their feet. The march continued – at a far slower pace now – and another five hours of constant darkness passed before they saw the light of the car ahead.

'Point your lights at it – everyone,' Pere said. 'We don't want to be run down.'

The driver, a robot, had been driving at half speed, watching for them. They climbed wearily aboard and most of them fell asleep during the short run back to HQ. The adjutant made a report to Pere.

'The break has been reported, and there have been two more blockages discovered in the other tunnel.'

'What caused them?'

'Intelligence is not sure, but is expecting to report soon.'

Pere swallowed his opinion of Intelligence's intelligence, since even robots should not hear morale-lowering comment. He pulled at his sticky shirt and was suddenly aware of the rising heat inside the car. 'What's wrong with the air conditioning?' he asked petulantly.

'Nothing, sir. It is the air temperature in the tunnel, it is much hotter than usual.'

'Why?'

'That fact is not known yet.'

The heat rose steadily as they approached HQ, and Pere issued orders that collars could be opened. The car slowed to a halt in the immense bay at the tunnel's end. When the door was opened the hot air that boiled in was almost unbreathable.

'Double-time to the lock,' Pere gasped out, choking over the words as the heat seared his throat. They stumbled and ran towards the large sealed valve at the end of the platform, robot guns tracking them from the turrets that studded the face of the metal wall. Identification was made and before they reached the lock the immense outer door rotated ponderously. Someone screamed as he fell and bare flesh touched the burning metal of the platform. Pere forced himself to wait until they were all inside, entering last. There was some relief when the outer door had closed, but no real drop in the temperature until they had passed through all five seals of the four-barreled lock. Even then the air inside the fortress was far warmer than normal.

'Perhaps this heat has something to do with the reason we were sent out a week early,' General Natia said. 'This and the tunnel blockage might be caused by an Enemy penetration in force.'

Pere had reached the same conclusion himself, though he wouldn't admit it aloud, even to his second-in-command. In addition only he knew that a real emergency at HQ had changed their shipping orders, though Command had not been specific about the nature of the emergency. As fast as he could, without running, Pere led his staff towards HQ control.

Nothing was right. No one answered him when he formally requested permission to enter. There were maintenance robots stolidly going about their work, but no officers in view. For a single heart-stopping instant he thought that all four battle stations were vacant. Then he saw a finger come out and touch a button at Command Prime: the occupant of the chair was slumped so low that he could hardly be seen. Pere stalked quickly towards the post and began a salute, but his hand stopped before it reached his forehead and forgotten, dropped slowly back. He stared with horror.

In the chair the operator gradually became aware that someone was standing over him. It was an effort for the man to draw the attention of his deep-socketed and reddened eyes from the board. When he did it was just for an instant and Pere had only a glimpse of the pain in their depths, of eyes peeping out of their black-rimmed pits like frightened animals. Then their attention wavered back to the board and the thin arm lifted tremulously to touch a control.

'Thank God you've come ... you've come at last ...

thank....' The words, scarcely a whisper to begin with, died away to a wheeze.

The officer's arms were pocked and scarred with needle holes: streaked with hardened rivulets of blood. The jumbled cartons and vials on the table told a wordless story of a man forcing himself to stay awake and active long past human limits: there were stimulants, sleep-surrogate, glucose, anesthetics, vitamin complexes. He had obviously been days alone in this chair, manning all four battle stations hooked into his own board. Alone – for some unknown and terrible reason alone – he had fought the war, waiting for help. With an uncontrollable feeling of revulsion Pere saw that the man had soiled himself as he sat there.

'General Natia, man that free board,' he ordered.

She slipped efficiently into the chair and set up a repeater from the others. Quickly taking in the factors of the conflict she called out, 'Ready, sir.'

Pere threw the command switch and the red bulb winked out on the board before him, and the one in front of Natia flashed on.

It was as though the light had been the spark of life holding the man at the controls. When the red bulb snuffed out he dropped his face into his hands and collapsed sideways into the cushioning chair. Pere took him by the shoulder and shook him until the hands dropped away and the last traces of consciousness stiffened the lolling head. With painful effort the man opened his eyes.

'What happened?' Pere asked. 'Where is everyone else?'

'Dead,' the feeble voice whispered, near to death itself. 'I was the only one didn't die – in bed at the time. Just chance I wasn't touching any metal. Just sheets, mattress. Robots say it was a vibration source – subsonic – supersonic – something new. Curdled everyone, killed them – coagulated the protein. Like eggs ... cooked eggs ... all dead.'

When the man sank into unconsciousness again Pere signalled to the medical officer who was standing by. Pere looked down at the solid steel floor beneath his feet and shuddered; the vibration weapon might be used again at any time. Or could it? The robots must have taken some preventative measures. He turned to the command robot, standing with steady metallic patience by the computer bank. Shaped like a normal motile, this robot's unique function was apparent only by the large vision screen on its chest and the thick cable, a metallic umbilical cord, that ran back from it to the computers behind. It was simply an extension of the giant computers and logic and memory units that were the heart of HQ.

'Have you found out what generated the killing vibration?' Pere asked the command robot.

'A machine that assembled and attached itself to the outer wall of HQ. It was detected as soon as it began operating and the frequencies were analyzed and neutralized in three minutes and seventeen seconds. No equipment or robots were injured since the frequencies used only caused resonance in animal protein. All of the staff, with the exception of Colonel Frey, were killed instantly. Large quantities of food in the lockers—'

'We'll concern ourselves with the food later. Where is the machine?'

'There,' the robot said, pointing towards the far wall. It led the way, its cable trailing smoothly behind it, and pulled a cover from the yard-high object resting there. It resembled no machine Pere had ever seen, rather it looked like a tangled mass of tiny gleaming roots: the red earth still packed between them heightened the illusion.

'How does it work?'

The robot reached out – leaning very close to focus its microscopic eyepieces – and carefully pulled one of the strands free. It lay on the robot's outstretched metallic palm, eight inches long, an eighth of an inch in diameter. Seen close it was not completely flexible, but made instead of pivoted and smoothly finished segments. The robot pointed out the parts of interest.

'The vibration generator is made up of a large number of

these machines, all of similar construction. At the front end is a hard-edged orifice that drills a hole in the ground. Debris is carried back through the body of the machine and eliminated here: in operation it is not unlike the common earthworm. Directional apparatus here guides it, orientated by a gravimeter to locate our base. Here a power unit and here a frequency generator. Singly the machines are harmless, their radiation of no importance. But when grouped together and activated at the same time they produce the deadly frequency.'

'Why weren't they detected before going into operation?'

'Their individual mass is too small and they have no metallic components. In addition they move very slowly, it took them a long time to reach HQ and mass for the attack.'

'How long?'

'By measuring the sensitivity of their gravimeters in response to the bulk of HQ and timing their speed of movement, it has been estimated that they entered the ground four years ago.'

'Four years!' General Pere was aghast at the thought. The miles of dirt and rock that surrounded HQ on all sides, formerly so comforting, changed suddenly to the hiding place of countless crawling, remorseless machines, closing in with mechanical patience.

'Can they be stopped from constructing another group-machine?'

'That is no problem now that it is known what we must guard against. Defensive screens and detectors have been installed.'

Anxiety seeped slowly away and Pere wiped the trickling sweat from his face as he looked around at his staff. All of the battle stations were manned now and the collapsed form of Colonel Frey had been taken out. Everything was functioning perfectly – except for the damn heat.

'And what's causing that?' Pere snapped. 'Why the rise in temperature? You must have found the cause.'

'The increased temperature is caused by areas of intense

heat in the soil around this station. The cause of this localized heat increase is unknown.'

Pere found himself worrying his thumb nail with his front teeth and angrily jerked it from his mouth. 'Cause unknown! I should think it would be obvious. If the Enemy can build complex wave generators into something as small as this piece of plastic spaghetti, they can certainly build more of them with some kind of compact heat generator. These things could be coming in in a second wave after the coagulator generators.'

'This theory was considered, as well as other high probability explanations, but we have no evidence...'

'Then get evidence!' Pere was angry at the persistant logicality of all robots, no matter how theoretically brilliant they might be. This obvious explanation of the mysterious heat seemed to him to be more than a hunch or guess, it was almost a certainty. He thumbed the button labeled IMPLEMENT ORDER on the robot's chest and issued a command. 'Search will be made at once beyond the heat zone to uncover any more of these specialized boring machines.'

With his defense taken care of he turned his attention to the war. Operations were proceeding so smoothly that the knot of tension in his midriff softened a bit. Lights flickered across the control boards, coded symbols for logistics and intelligence. The operators collated and questioned, feeding their results to Command Prime where General Natia sat relaxed yet completely alert. The electronic war of course moved at too great a pace for the human mind to follow. All of the missiles, anti-missile missiles, interceptors, bombers and tank squadrons were robot-controlled and -operated. Computers of varying degrees of intelligence and responsibility did the actual battle ordering. The same was true of logistics. But men had started this war and guided it towards its finish. The human operators made sense of the shifting factors in the global battle and chose the best course from among those fed to them by the strategy machines. The war had been going well. Analysis of the results showed a small increment of victory during the past nine months. If this increment could be kept steady – or even increased – another generation or two might see complete victory. It was a pleasant, though slightly disconcerting, thought for Pere.

Five shifts later the first of the thermal-wrigglers was found and neutralized. Pere examined it with distaste. So small to be causing so much trouble. They were all wearing tropical kit now, and constantly uncomfortable in the overheated air. The only external difference between this wriggler and the wave generators was in the color of its plastic body; the new one was an appropriately fiery red.

'How does it generate the heat?' Pere asked the command robot.

'The machine contains a suicide circuit. The power supply is short circuited through a contractile field. The circuits burn out in microseconds, but there is enough time to compress a small quantity of hydrogen—'

'It implodes! A small hydrogen bomb?'

'In a sense, yes. There is very little radiation, most of the energy is released as heat. A molten pocket of lava is the result. The heat dissipates slowly into our base here. New implosions add constantly to the molten area outside.'

'Can't you detect and destroy these things before they detonate?'

'This is difficult because of the large number of them involved and the volume of earth that must be inspected. Special machines and detectors are being constructed. An extrapolation has been made of all the factors, and it is estimated with a ninety-nine percent certainty that the heat will not rise to the point where it interferes with the operation of the base.'

This was one load of worry that Pere could cheerfully throw aside: the constant heat was a continual source of discomfort to them all. He wondered idly just how hot it would get before the temperature started back down.

'What is your estimate of this maximum temperature?' he asked.

'Five hundred degrees,' the robot said with mechanical imperturbability.

Pere stared into the blank eye cells of the machine and had the sensation of being suddenly hammered down and gasping for air. 'Why – that's five times higher than the boiling temperature of water!'

'That is correct. Water boils at one hundred degrees.'

Pere could only choke with unbelief. 'Do you realize what you are saying? What do you think people are ... How can we live?'

The robot did not answer since this problem was not the responsibility of the HQ robots. Pere chewed his lip and rephrased it.

'This temperature is unsatisfactory for the personnel – even if the machines can survive it. You must find some way to lower the temperature.'

'This problem has already been considered, since a number of the more delicate components will be near their critical range at that temperature. The air conditioning units are now operating at maximum overload and no new units can be added. Therefore drilling operations have begun and are tapping nearby deposits of water, which will be substituted for air within the base. This water will enter at a lower temperature and will have a greater heat transfer capacity.'

A compromise, not a perfect answer, but it might work for awhile. One room would have to be sealed off for living quarters and the watch officers could wear pressure suits. Uncomfortable but not impossible.

'What will be the maximum temperature of this water?' he asked.

'One hundred and forty degrees. There is adequate water to bring the temperature lower, but this base was not designed for easy circulation of anything other than air. All machine units are of battle standard and waterproof—'

'People aren't!' Pere shouted, forgetting himself. 'And if they were they would cook in this boiling soup of yours. How are we to survive, tell me that?'

Once more the oracle was silent. In the distance there was the sudden gush and spatter of water.

'What's that?' he gasped.

'Flooding. The lower levels,' the robot said.

Everyone in the room was watching him, Pere realized, listening to the final judgment of the robot's words. 'Anyone have any ideas?' he asked, unaware of the pleading in his voice. There were no answers.

There had to be an answer; he forced his numbed mind to check over the possibilities. Remote control of HQ from National Central? No, too dangerous, control circuits could be interrupted, cut off or even taken over. Someone had to be here, at least one person to man the Command Prime station. Unless this station could be robot-controlled too.

'A discretion circuit,' he shouted with sudden relief. 'Can a robot with discretion circuitry be built to operate the Command station?' he asked the robot extension of HQ.

'Yes.'

'Well do it. Do it at once. We may have to evacuate, and in case we do I want the robot ready to take over.'

It wouldn't be for long, they would just be gone until the temperature dropped and human habitation became possible again. All of the decisions to be made at Command Prime were simple *either-or* choices, and an occasional multiple choice. A robot with the correct evaluation and discretion circuits would do well enough for awhile. It wouldn't be perfect and the victory increment would surely drop a few points, but it wouldn't be disaster. He would have to check with National Central before putting the plan into operation, but he was sure they wouldn't come up with a better answer.

They didn't. The aging commanders couldn't even do as well and were grateful to General Pere for the suggestion. He even received a promotion and was authorized to wear another star on his shoulder. As soon as the command robot could begin satisfactory operation he was ordered to evacuate.

On the lower levels the hot oily water reached to their

knees. The tension among the staff ebbed away only when the new robot was carried in. Pere watched and frowned when the machine was bolted into place in his chair. The job had been a quick one and no special care had been taken with unessentials; the body of the robot consisted simply of a square box, ugly with beaded weld marks. Two eye cells sat on a stubby column above it and a single, articulated arm projected from the front. The eyes focused on the unlit command light and the arm hung down limply. Pere had all the other boards tied into the logistics board, took one last look at the war, then decisively threw the command switch.

The red light came on in front of the robot and it instantly began operation. With lightning speed the metallic index finger pressed three buttons and threw a switch, then drooped again. Pere looked at the decisions and could find no fault. Perhaps he might have brought in the reserve tanks in the eastern bulge and tried to hold. Though it was just as tactically sound to withdraw and straighten the line and save on the estimated losses. Both choices had the same probability rating on the scale, which was why they had appeared on the board. The robot would work.

He hated it though. For some reason it seemed a colossal personal affront to him to be replaced by this arm-waving black box. Was this all that a man was to a machine? The metal fingers ran across the controls, then dropped again.

'Prepare to move out,' he shouted in a harsh voice. This evacuation was wrong, very wrong. But what else could he do?

'We'll rig a stretcher for Colonel Frey,' he told the medical officer. 'How is he progressing?'

'He's dead,' the doctor said with his toneless professional manner. 'The heat was too much for him in his weakened condition. Too much of a strain on his heart.'

'Alright,' Pere said, keeping his emotions under control. 'That leaves Zen as the only casualty and he can walk well enough with his arm in a cast.'

When the officers had all assembled General Natia stepped up to Pere and saluted. 'All present, sir. Everyone is carrying extra rations and water, in case there is trouble in the return tunnel.'

'Yes, of course,' Pere said, mentally berating himself for not thinking of these simple precautions. There had been so much on his mind. It was time to leave.

'Has the mono tunnel been kept open?' he asked the adjutant.

'Two additional minor blockages have occurred, but have been cleared.'

'Very good. Fall in with the others. Attention ... right face ... forward MARCH.' As his small company tramped out of the room General Pere turned back, goaded by some anachronistic impulse, and saluted the command post. None of the machines paid the slightest attention to him. The robot in his chair jabbed a quick finger at some buttons and ignored him. Feeling slightly foolish he turned quickly and followed the others out.

They were cycling through the multiple sealed doors of the fortress when they met the robot. It was waiting in the outer compartment and pushed past them as soon as the door was open. It was a worker, a mechanical of some kind, scratched and covered with mud: because it had no speech facilities Pere had to question it through the adjutant.

'Find out what has happened,' he snapped.

The two robots held a voiceless communion, their radio waves in a direct brain-to-brain hookup carried thoughts far faster than could any speech.

'The exit tunnel has been blocked,' the adjutant said. 'The roof is down in many places and it is beginning to fill with water. The decision has been reached that it cannot be opened. New falls are occurring all the time.'

'Challenge the decision. It is not possible,' Pere said. There was a note of desperation in his voice.

They were through the last door now and in the exit bay. The heat was overpowering and made intelligent thought almost impossible. Through a red haze Pere saw bulky digging robots streaming out of the mouth of the exit tunnel, going towards the entrance valve behind them.

'No change is possible,' the adjutant said, a metallic voice of doom. 'The tunnel cannot be opened now. It has been found that small machines, very like the heat units, have penetrated the earth and are collapsing the tunnel. It will be opened after they—'

'Another way! There must be another way out!' Pere's voice was as heat-strained as his thoughts, yet the robot understood and took it for a command.

'There are emergency exits here that once led to higher levels. My information is incomplete. I do not know if they have been sealed.'

'Show us – we can't stay here.'

They were all wearing gloves, so the metal bars of the ladder didn't char their hands, just burned them. The robot adjutant went first and only his mechanical strength could have turned the time-sealed wheel that locked the entrance to the older levels. The humans groped their way behind the adjutant, some falling and failing to rise again. Colonel Zen must have been the first to be left behind because he only had the use of one arm. The heat in the stifling darkness was so great that even the doctor didn't notice when his patient dropped out. The doctor himself must have gone soon after, because he was no longer a young man.

General Pere tried to issue orders, and when they were not obeyed he made an attempt to help the laggards himself. He could not do this and keep up with the others. When he saw the lights winking out of sight in the dust-filled passage ahead, he made the only decision possible under the circumstances. Not that he was aware of making it, he was barely conscious at the time and only the will to survive drove him forward. Passing the straggling survivors he shouldered General Natia aside and took his place behind the guiding robot.

Pain fought a battle with fatigue and kept them going until they were out of the zone of terrible heat. Pere had strength enough only to utter the one-word command to stop, drink from his canteen, then fall unconscious to the floor. The others dropped in huddled lumps of pain about him. The adjutant stood with untiring machine-patience, waiting for them to rise.

Moans of agony roused Pere at last and he forced his charred fingers to fumble out the first-aid packs. Burn ointment brought some relief to the five survivors and stimulants gave them the illusion of strength needed to carry on. General Natia had somehow managed to stay close behind him through the ordeal, as well as three others. They were all young and strong, though one was not strong enough. He simply vanished during the next climb.

Above HQ was a maze of tunnels and rooms, occupied by the base at various times before the unremitting pressures of the war had driven the controllers even deeper into the ground. Most of it was collapsed and choked with rubble and no progress was possible. If the robot had not been with them they would have died. Every detail of the various layers was impressed in his electronical cortex, since his brain contained the memory of every other adjutant back to the beginning of the war. They retraced their steps whenever their way was blocked and found a different direction. Bit by bit they progressed towards the surface. There was no way to measure time in the darkness; they slept when exhaustion was too great, then woke up to stumble on. Their food was gone and the water almost exhausted. They kept going only because of the robot's firm insistence that they were now in the upper levels.

'We are just under the surface of the ground,' the adjutant said. 'This tunnel led to a gun position, but it is now blocked.'

Pere sat and blinked at the circular tunnel and forced his fatigued brain to consider the problem. The top of the tunnel was not much higher than their heads and made of ferro-concrete. Jagged chunks of the same material choked the end.

'Clear away the opening,' Pere ordered.

'I cannot,' the robot said. 'My battery is almost discharged, I would not be able to finish.'

This was the end. They could not go on.

'Perhaps we could ... blow it out of the way,' Natia said apologetically. Pere turned his light on her and she shook a handful of cartridges from the clip at her waist. 'These contain powerful explosive. Perhaps the adjutant could arrange them to all explode together.'

'I can,' the adjutant said.

Surprisingly, all four of them still had their sidearms and spare clips; they had not been discarded with the rest of the equipment. The adjutant took the spare clips and buried them in the rubble while they moved back down the tunnel. A minute later the robot came running back to join them and they pressed themselves to the floor. The ground jumped and the roar of concussion smote their ears. They forced themselves to wait long minutes for the stifling cloud of dust to settle, before Pere let them go forward.

The barrier was still there, but the ceiling had fallen and high up in the gap a ray of light shone on the dust motes.

'We're through,' Pere said hoarsely. 'Help me up there.'

Steadied by the robot he reached up into the hole and crumbled away the soft dirt at the lip until it was big enough for his shoulders. A lump came away with a tuft of grass, green and damp. He groped up through the hole, reaching for a hold.

'Let me help you,' a voice said, and brown calloused hands clutched his and pulled.

It was so unexpected that Pere gasped wth shock. Yet he could not let go and the hand pulled him steadily out of the hole in the ground. He fell face first onto the grass and groped for his gun, while the light burned into his eyes. Through tears of pain he saw a circle of legs surrounding him, and took his hand from the pistol butt.

The others were out of the hole now and as his eyes adjusted Pere could look around him. The sky was cloudy and it must have been raining because the grass on which he sat was damp. Before him stretched a freshly plowed field. He felt a sudden spurt of pleasure at identifying these things that he had only seen before on the screen. This was the first time in his life that he had ever been above ground.

Of course all of the recordings he had seen were historicals, from the time before the war when people still lived on the surface, instead of in the numerous sub-cities. He had always assumed that the surface was sterile and bare of life. Then who were these people? Something whistled and screamed away into the distance over his head, and he was aware for the first time of a constant rumbling that seemed to come from all sides.

'Who are you?' a voice asked, and Pere struggled up to face the man who had helped him from the hole.

'I am General Pere, this is my staff.' The man had a very dark skin and was wearing a weird costume that seemed to consist completely of cast-off mechanical items. His tunic was plexicloth from a machine cover: his shoes wedges of metal with webbing straps to hold them in place. He wore a metal helmet on his head as did all the others.

'A general,' the man grunted and the smile vanished from his face. He turned and whistled shrilly. In the field there were some more people pulling at a strange device, one of them waved and they started in Pere's direction.

'Boruk is coming,' the tan-skinned man said gruffly. 'Talk to him. Maybe it'll do some good. Though I doubt it.' He spat on the ground and kicked dirt into the spittle with one toe.

Overhead in the clouds there was a muffled and gigantic explosion. Pere looked up and saw the clouds briefly stained a rosy pink. A black speck appeared below the clouds and before his horrified eyes grew instantly to the shape of a giant wheel. It plunged down, apparently at him, but hit instead on the far side of the field. The huge tire recoiled and it bounced into the air directly over their heads. Only Pere and his officers looked up as it sailed over. The wheel must have been a hundred feet in diameter and he could see clearly the treads on the tire, and the metal hub with its sheared supports, a stream of liquid still leaking from some severed pipe. It bounced again, shaking the ground, and vanished from sight over the hill.

'What was that?' Pere asked, but no one answered him.

The group in the field were closer now and he could see they were pulling a plow assembled of odd pieces of junk. The two handles of the plow were the only identifiable parts: the arms of a robot welded into place, the hands extended and acting as handles. One of the men who had been tugging in a harness dropped it and walked over. He was naked to the waist, but wore a pair of gray uniform pants and high boots.

'The military!' he shouted when he saw their uniforms. 'Wonderful! Wonderful!' He turned and ran away. A fine rain of metallic particles hit the grass around them. Pere had the feeling he was going mad.

The man had only gone to the side of the field to get the rest of his clothes. He struggled into a jacket and in place of his steel helmet pulled on a peaked cap of hauntingly familiar design. Only when he had buttoned it and knocked the dust from his trousers did he turn and come towards Pere.

'The Enemy!' Pere shouted and scratched for his gun. This was the uniform he had seen so many times in orientation films. He hauled the gun out but someone knocked it from his fingers. Then he could only stand paralyzed as the man stamped up to him, clicked his heels together and saluted.

'General Boruk,' he said. 'On a mission of peace. May I ask whom I have the pleasure of addressing?' He dropped the salute and pulled a white flag from one pocket with a collapsible rod attached to it. After snapping open the rod he held the flag up proudly. His face was as sunburned as the others, with a black moustache and pointed beard.

'I am General Pere,' Pere forced himself to say. 'Who are you? What are you doing here?'

'At your service, general,' Boruk said, and stabbed the pole into the ground. He groped in another pocket and fished out a large wallet. 'I bring you greetings from my proud country, and the joyous news that we wish to sue for peace. All of the papers are here – including my credentials

– and you have only to forward them to the proper authorities. You will notice that there is mention of a peace commission, but I am forced to admit that they are all dead or have returned. In fact, to be truthful, you will see my name entered on the rolls of the commission as Captain Boruk, but this was only in the beginning. Through determination and the fact I am young and strong as a bull, I was promoted to dizzying heights. In fact General Graniaz, who himself conferred my commission upon me, even gave me his own coat with his general's insignia. In that, his was a wise choice, for I ask you only to notice that I am here and the others are not. We want peace, any terms you care to name. Do you agree?'

'Sit down,' Pere said, feeling the need to do so himself. 'Why are you asking for peace now – allowing for the moment that your credentials are not forged? You are not losing the war?'

'To be truthful again, general, we are not even fighting the war.' Boruk sprawled on the ground and chewed a stem of grass. 'You will discover the reason for our request sooner or later, so it might as well be sooner. In fact sooner the better since the situation is so far out of hand. It seems we have been forced to abandon our battle headquarters and turn it over to robot operation. Are you all right?' he asked, seeing Pere jump.

'Yes,' Pere told him. 'Yes, go on.' This was too familiar to permit him to listen easily.

'I must say your scientists are tricky ones, I believe they managed to invest our HQ with a mutated virus that was impossible to eradicate. The base had to be evacuated, radiated and sterilized. To do this the robots had to be left in complete control of the war operations. When we tried to get back in, it was most difficult. All entrances had been sealed and we couldn't get the robots to understand what we wanted. They were doing very well without us, very well indeed.' He spat the grass out and scowled.

'But there are ways. You could have countermanded—'

'It is not that easy, general. I assure you we tried. To be

brief, the more we tried the better the robot defenses against our interferences became. In the end they fought us off – having identified us with the Enemy – and we had to retire.'

'*We'll* get back in,' Pere said, then snapped his mouth shut guiltily.

'I had assumed something of the sort,' Boruk smiled. His seemingly lazy attention had missed nothing. 'When a general and his staff climb out of the ground above the area of their HQ, I am afraid I leaped to a conclusion due to my own previous knowledge. Is it true? You have been forced to leave as well?'

'I'll tell you nothing.'

'You don't have to. It is a cosmic jest indeed.' Boruk laughed humorlessly and tore the surrender papers across and threw them into the dirt. Something keened through the air and exploded in an immense cloud of dust on the horizon. 'You have been pushed out the way our officers were pushed out, and you shall not get back. It was due to come, since every other part of the battle in this war is done by robots. Since we have both been concentrating our weapons upon the opposite headquarters, it was fated that some of the weapons should have at least a partial success. Robots are much stronger than humans, much more able to stand lethal climates. I have had plenty of time to think about this, since I have waited here many months.'

'Why – why didn't you surrender? Why didn't you come to us?'

'Believe me, my young companion general, that is the one wish of my country. But how is this done in this day of total war? We tried radio and all other forms of communication, but all were blocked by robot mechanisms designed for that job. Then we sent the mission in person – not carrying weapons, so of course the robots ignored us. Our casualties were due simply to the deadliness of the battlefields we had to cross on the way here. The robots were completely indifferent to us, a forewarning of the future – or of the present, I might say. Battle is going on everywhere, and only a few peaceful areas exist, such as this one, above a strongly defended base. But even when I reached here I found no surface installations and no way of reaching you below.'

'This is monstrous! Monstrous!' Pere bellowed.

'It is indeed, but we must be philosophical about it. Accept it as these good people have done who live here under a canopy of death. The robots will continue their war just as efficiently without us, and probably make it last much longer since they are so evenly matched. Find yourself a woman, settle down and enjoy the life.'

Pere found himself glancing inadvertently at Natia, who looked away and blushed. Even if she was a general, she had a fine figure. . . .

'No!' he shouted. 'I will not submit. This is terrible. This is no way for mankind to live. Just to sit by and watch these senseless machines destroy each other.'

'It does not matter, friend general, whether we like it or not. We have been bypassed. Displaced. We have played too long at the destructive game of war and made our machines too efficient. They enjoy the game too much themselves to relinquish it, and we must find some place where we can try and live to the best of our abilities. Some place where they will not step on us while they play.'

'No, I can't accept it!' Pere shouted again and tears of frustration and anger burned in his eyes. He threw off Natia's hand when she put it on his arm. The horizon grumbled and flared red, hot metal rattled into the ground nearby.

'I just hope you're having a good time,' he cried and shook his fist up at the unheeding sky. 'I just hope you're having a good time!'

The world's greatest science fiction authors now available in Panther Books

Bob Shaw

The Ceres Solution	£1.50	☐
A Better Mantrap	£1.50	☐
Orbitsville	£1.95	☐
Orbitsville Departure	£1.95	☐

William Burroughs

Nova Express	£1.25	☐

Arthur C Clarke

2010: Odyssey Two	£1.95	☐

Harry Harrison

Rebel in Time	£1.95	☐

The To The Stars Trilogy

Homeworld	£1.95	☐
Wheelworld	£1.95	☐
Starworld	£1.95	☐

James Kahn

World Enough, and Time	£1.95	☐
Time's Dark Laughter	£1.95	☐

Christopher Stasheff

A Wizard in Bedlam	£1.25	☐
The Warlock in Spite of Himself	£1.25	☐
King Kobold	£1.50	☐
The Warlock Unlocked	£1.95	☐

Doris Lessing
'Canopus in Argos: Archives'

Shikasta	£2.50	☐
The Marriage Between Zones Three, Four, and Five	£1.95	☐
The Sirian Experiments	£1.95	☐
The Making of the Representative for Planet 8	£1.95	☐

David Mace

Demon 4	£1.50	☐
Nightrider	£1.95	☐

To order direct from the publisher just tick the titles you want and fill in the order form.

All these books are available at your local bookshop or newsagent, or can be ordered direct from the publisher.

To order direct from the publisher just tick the titles you want and fill in the form below.

Name_____

Address _____

_____

Send to:
Panther Cash Sales
PO Box 11, Falmouth, Cornwall TR10 9EN.

Please enclose remittance to the value of the cover price plus:

UK 45p for the first book, 20p for the second book plus 14p per copy for each additional book ordered to a maximum charge of £1.63.

BFPO and Eire 45p for the first book, 20p for the second book plus 14p per copy for the next 7 books, thereafter 8p per book.

Overseas 75p for the first book and 21p for each additional book.

Panther Books reserve the right to show new retail prices on covers, which may differ from those previously advertised in the text or elsewhere.